Grandparent Trap

The Family Game

by
Carollee Young

Dedicated to
CHARLEE ANNE

Chapter 1

Setup

Laura Blaine looked in the rear view mirror and glanced at her youngest child, Andrew. He was almost three years old with curly, dark blond hair that was a magnet for grape bubble gum. He had mastered the art of chewing gum at a very early age and it kept his small mouth so busy he never bothered to talk. When someone would try to get him to talk he would close his eyes, pucker up his lips, and turn his face away from the annoying person. He looked quite sickly with his thin face, purple lips, and solemn blue eyes. Laura worried about her little guy, concerned with his appearance and the fact that he was not talking. She had taken him to several doctors, but they all diagnosed him as a healthy child and said, "He will talk when he has something to say."

Laura said to her four children, "Okay, we're almost there. Are you ready for this? Do we need to go over anything before I drop you off?"

"No, Mom. We've been practicing for months. I think we know what to do," said Dawn.

Dawn liked to take charge of what was going on in her life. She was a straight-A student and every spare minute she had was spent reading a book. Her mother took her to the library each Tuesday so she would have books to read during the week. At her reading pace, she had lost interest in the books the girls her age were reading. Dawn would pass up the children's section in the library and head for "the more interesting books" as she put it. The last book she read was about a near-death experience. Quite a mature subject for a girl of twelve, but she was captivated with what she had read. She even wrote to the author to ask if he knew of any soldiers serving in the Middle East having a near-death experience. The author was fascinated that a twelve-year-old had taken an interest in his book so he personally wrote back to her. He told her that he hadn't done any research on soldiers but maybe he would for his next book.

Dawn didn't look like either of her parents and they always wondered where she inherited her strawberry-blond hair. The only feature she had of her dad's was a small purple diamond-shaped birthmark on the inside of her left ankle. Dawn cherished it because it was a remembrance of her father. For the most part she was content with her life—except for her thrift-shop clothes.

Laura looked over at her oldest son. He was sitting in the front passenger seat. "Shawn, you know what to do if anything goes wrong and you've memorized the phone number, right?"

"Mom, how many times have I called the number? This is the third year we've done this."

He had the same curly, dark blond hair as his brother. They had both inherited it from their father. He had Laura's brown eyes with long eyelashes. His nose was just a little crooked but you couldn't tell unless you really looked close.

When he was eight, he was playing center field in a neighborhood baseball game when the batter hit the ball straight to him. He put his glove up to catch the ball, but closed his eyes against the blinding sun. The ball missed his glove and hit him square in the face. It knocked him to the ground with blood streaming out of his nose. When he regained consciousness, his mother was sitting beside him holding his hand. He looked at her in bewilderment and asked, "Where are we? I hear sirens."

"We're in an ambulance on our way to the hospital. You got hit with the ball and it knocked you out. I think it broke your nose!" she said as she put his hand to her lips and kissed the back of it.

"I didn't catch the ball," he said, obviously disappointed, but in the same breath said, "Are we really in an ambulance?" He tried to sit up. "Can I look out the window?"

He was so like his father, paying no mind to the danger but looking for the adventure. The broken nose did not deter his love for baseball or the desire to play the game. He was mature for a twelve-year-old, something that was forced on him three years ago. He also had acquired a not-so-pleasant attitude on occasion, which concerned his mother.

"Mommy, do you think they'll like me? I don't think the last grandma liked me very much," Kimber said, with a pouting face.

"She did like you," said Dawn "but I think this one will like you even better."

Two years ago, when the family started what they called "The Family Game," Kimberly was five. Now at seven, she insisted on being called "Kimber." She said it sounded like a ballerina's name and she was going to be a ballerina. She looked just like her mother. She had the same brown eyes, perfect nose, and full lips that she turned in and squeezed together when she was concentrating on her dancing. Laura had found a pair of pink ballerina shoes at the thrift store along with tights, leotard, and tutu. Kimber had out-grown several dancing outfits and Laura was always lucky enough to find others. It was as if they were waiting to belong to Kimber.

Because money was so limited, Laura had no choice but to shop at thrift stores to dress her children. In fact, most everything they owned was from a thrift store. Kimber didn't mind the hand-me-down clothes; she would entertain the family by making up stories about where each of her outfits had been and who had owned them. She was a happy child for the most part. The only thing that bothered her was she couldn't take ballet lessons. There just wasn't enough money in the budget.

"Okay, we're only a few houses away," said Laura as she pulled the car to a stop. This part of the game was always so hard for Laura and she was close to tears. "You know we don't have to go through with this."

"Oh, Mom, it's only a game and we'll be fine," Dawn said impatiently. Although Dawn put on a confident act, she did have butterflies in her stomach.

"You children are so good. How can you be so calm? I'm always such a wreck at this point." Laura hugged and kissed each child as they got out of the car holding their small, worn-out suitcases filled with their best clothes. As she watched them walk away she called to them, "Make sure you watch after the little ones! Especially Andrew! It's his first time!"

Dawn handed Andrew a worn-out teddy bear. He threw it on the ground. Dawn picked it up and handed it to him again whispering something in his ear. This time he didn't throw it but dragged it behind him.

"You call me anytime," Laura called. She was following them about two house-lengths behind them.

Shawn turned around, walked back to his mother, wrapped his arms around her and said, "Mom, we'll be fine. You have a wonderful vacation." He turned and caught up with his siblings.

4

Laura watched them walk up to the porch of a house, tears filling her eyes. She went back to the car and didn't drive away until she saw them disappear into the house.

Chapter 2

Surprise

It was almost 9 p.m. when the doorbell rang. Janet Chapman was in the kitchen making cookies and her husband was sitting in his recliner watching a baseball game. "Warren, would you get that? I'm up to my elbows in cookie dough."

Warren had not heard the doorbell or his wife because he had dozed off—as usual. He was spending too much time in his recliner watching TV and sleeping since he retired. He didn't want to retire, but the architectural firm he worked for had been sold and the new owners were young and had fresh, new ideas. All the older architects were offered a retirement package too good to refuse. It had been six months now and he was not doing well with the transition from working over forty hours a week to doing nothing, despite all the encouragement from his family to find a hobby. He didn't want to play golf because at his age, he couldn't see himself starting a sport he never had an interest in. The family dragged him out bowling several times trying to get him to join a league. It didn't work. "Bowling is too noisy," he said. He always had an excuse for not doing every hobby the family thought up and suggested to him.

The doorbell rang again. "Warren, would you get the door? Someone is at the door!" Janet said a little louder this time.

His wife's voice brought him out of his sleep. "What did you say?"

"The doorbell. Go and see who is at the door!" she shot back.

"I can't. I'm busy," he said in a groggy voice.

"Oh, for goodness' sake," she said as she popped a sheet of cookies in the oven.

Janet was quite surprised when she found four children standing at her door. "Isn't it a little late to be out selling something? It's almost dark."

"We're not selling anything. Are you Mrs. Chapman?" asked Dawn.

Surprised that the young girl knew her name, Janet asked. "How do you know my name? And if you're not selling anything, why are you here?"

"Your daughter, April, volunteered to take care of us for a while," said Shawn, not wanting to let his sister do all the talking. Dawn was five minutes older than Shawn and she always assumed she was in charge. But three years ago, he was told he was now the man of the house.

Janet was dumbfounded. "Where is your mother?" she demanded as she looked over their heads for any sign of her.

"She's on vacation," chirped Kimber. Janet glanced Kimber's way and found herself looking into the eyes of a little girl who was dressed in faded clothing. In fact, she noticed all the children looked like poor little orphans dressed in shabby clothes that fit poorly.

Linda, the Chapman's youngest daughter, joined her mother at the front door.

"Do you know anything about April taking care of children?" Janet asked Linda.

"No," said Linda, "but it's not unlike her. Remember when she invited her friend's children over to swim in the pool all day?"

Janet sighed in agreement and turned to the children. "April isn't here. She's somewhere in Africa, so you'll have to call your mother to come get you."

"I smell cookies," said Kimber.

"Oh, no! My cookies!" Janet blurted out as she ran into the kitchen to take the cookies out of the oven. "I hope they didn't burn."

"We'll eat them that way," Kimber said smiling at Janet. All the children had followed her into the kitchen. She looked into Kimber's sweet little face and melted. "*If I had a granddaughter,*" she thought, "*I would want her to be just like this little girl.*"

"Mom, I'm leaving now. I'll try to get in touch with April tomorrow."

"What shall I do with these children?" Janet asked her daughter.

"Do what you do best, Mom. Feed them cookies and milk, read them a bedtime story, and tuck them into bed. We can sort things out tomorrow."

"I guess one night wouldn't hurt," Janet said. In fact, the idea kind of appealed to her. It would be nice having little ones around the house again even if it was just for one night.

Janet's kitchen was all white with bright red and dark blue trim and matching accessories. The red gingham curtains and tablecloth gave it a cheery, cozy-country feeling.

"This is a very nice kitchen," said Kimber.

"What's your name and how old are you?" Janet asked as she gave Kimber two cookies and a glass of milk.

"My name is Kimber and I'm seven years old. Thank you for the cookies."

Janet smiled at Kimber and looked over at Dawn. "What's your name and how old are you?"

"I'm twelve, and my name is Dawn. This is my twin brother ,Shawn. I'm older than he is."

"You may be older but, I'm in charge and I can introduce myself." Shawn glared at his sister. "Mrs. Chapman, thank you for inviting us in for cookies."

"You are very welcome, Shawn," said Janet. She looked at Andrew. "And what is your name? I bet you're just about three years old."

Andrew made a face at Janet, turned up his nose, and hid his face in Dawn's side.

"His name is Andrew. He doesn't talk and he turns three in two months," answered Dawn.

She watched the children enjoying the warm cookies as they washed them down with milk. *"What kind of mother would just drop off her children, leave, and not stop to visit awhile," she thought.* Trying to bring up the subject of their mother, she asked, "Does your mother bake you cookies?"

"No, she doesn't have time because she works two jobs. She works during the day, full time, Monday through Friday, and she is a waitress Wednesday, Thursday, and Friday evenings and all day on Saturday. Then on Sunday we go to church," Dawn responded, munching on a cookie.

"Where is your father?" Janet asked.

"Our father was killed three years ago serving in Iraq," said Shawn biting his lower lip.

"Oh, you poor children," said Janet sympathetically.

"Dawn tries to make cookies, but she isn't very good at it. They turn out worse than these cookies," piped Kimber.

"Kimber, that's not very nice to say," said Dawn.

"It's true," said Shawn. "You're always reading some book or other. Maybe if you read a cookbook or two you'd cook better."

"Now children, don't fuss at each other," coached Janet. "Where is Andrew?"

They found Andrew curled up in Warren Chapman's lap sound asleep. "He brought me a cookie, climbed up onto my lap, and fell asleep. Who is he anyway?"

"He's our little brother, Andrew," said Shawn as he reached to lift him up. "I'll take him. Sorry if he bothered you, Mr. Chapman."

"It's getting late; I'll show you where you'll sleep," said Janet. She put the two boys in the bedroom that had been their son, Donnie's. Donnie was the Chapman's middle child. Warren had wanted Donnie to follow him in his own occupation and become an architect. Donnie did have an interest in architectural design, but he studied interior design in college and now worked for an interior design company in New York.

Janet put the girls in April's room since she was vacationing. April was the firstborn—very pretty and very independent. She wasn't much of a party girl. She would rather stay home and read a book on some far-away place she wanted to visit. She worked hard all year and saved her money and vacation time so she could take one long trip each year.

Janet was impressed with how the children brushed their teeth without being told. Shawn helped Andrew brush his teeth and put on his pajamas. They all had mismatched pajamas but their tooth-brushes looked new and they even brought their own toothpaste. She was amazed when all the children knelt down by one of the beds and Shawn said a prayer. She was overwhelmed by the wonderful warm feeling she had for these children that she had only known for about an hour. She couldn't help but kiss each child on the forehead, tuck them in, and say goodnight.

After a few minutes, Kimber whispered, "Dawn, are you asleep?"

"No, I'm still awake."

"This is a nice room. All the furniture matches!" said Kimber. "Did you see all the pictures on the walls?"

"Yes," Dawn said. "There's one of the Roman Coliseum and one of the Eiffel Tower in Paris, France."

"I like it here. Do you?" asked Kimber.

"Yes, I think it's going to be pleasant, but we still need to be careful. Now go to sleep, Kimber."

Shawn fought going to sleep as his little brother slept peacefully next to him. He waited until he couldn't hear any more movement in the house and heard what he thought was the sound of Warren's snoring. He slowly got out of bed, pulled out the phone, dialed the memorized number, and said in a hushed voice, "Mom we're fine. I think we'll like it here. Call you tomorrow."

Chapter 3

Stop, Don't Eat Yet!

Shaking her sister, Kimber said, "Dawn, are you awake? I smell bacon!"

"I've been awake for a while worried about what will happen today."

"Come on, let's go eat," Kimber said as she climbed out of bed.

"Kimber, we need to make our bed before we leave the room. Don't you remember what Mom said?"

"Okay, but let's do it fast. I'm hungry."

All the children reached the kitchen at the same time. On the table were a pitcher of orange juice, a plate of bacon, and a huge stack of pancakes. Warren was just getting ready to put a big bite of three-high pancakes, oozing with butter and hot maple syrup, into his mouth.

"Stop!" Kimber warned. "Don't eat yet."

Warren lowered his fork and shot a questioning glance at Kimber.

"We haven't said the morning prayer," said Kimber.

"Maybe Mr. and Mrs. Chapman don't participate in morning prayer," said Dawn.

"I think today is a good day to start," said Mrs. Chapman.

"Mr. Chapman, would you choose someone to say the prayer?" asked Shawn.

"Let me!" Kimber volunteered, waving her raised hand.

"I think that would be fine. After all, it was your idea," said Warren Chapman.

Andrew climbed into the chair next to Warren and took hold of Warren's big hand with his little one. Kimber bowed her head and started the prayer. "Dear Father in Heaven, thank you for letting us stay with this nice grandma and grandpa. Bless our daddy who is in heaven with you. Let Mommy have a fun vacation, and bless this food. In Jesus' name, amen."

Janet thought, *"How impressive and how much I like this little girl Kimber."*

"Warren," said Janet." I think we need to get a phone book for Andrew to sit on. He can barely see over the table."

The children were silent now; the only sound was the silverware clinking against the plates as everyone enjoyed a scrumptious breakfast.

Warren looked at Kimber, "In your prayer, which was a very good one, you said your father was in heaven. What happened to him?"

"My daddy is a hero; he died for his country," said Kimber with a sad face.

"Our father was a career soldier—a Staff Sergeant in the U.S. Army," said Dawn. "He was killed with several other soldiers when a roadside bomb exploded and demolished their Humvee in Iraq."

"I'm so sorry to hear that. He sounds like he was a very fine and honorable man," Warren tenderly replied.

Everyone's attention was drawn to Andrew. He started whimpering and beating his little fists on the table.

"Andrew, calm down," said Shawn. But Andrew just cried louder and pounded harder.

"He gets this way sometimes when we talk about our father. Mom found out she was pregnant with him the same day our father was killed. I think he somehow feels his father had to die so he could be born," said Dawn.

"Dawn, you don't know that. There you go again with that death stuff," Shawn said with disgust.

Andrew was now screaming and pounding the table with all his might.

"Will someone do something for him?" yelled Warren, "I can't stand the noise!"

"The only thing that will calm him down is grape bubblegum," shouted Shawn. "But our mom wouldn't let us pack any because he gets it in his hair!"

"Didn't Donnie like grape bubblegum, Janet?" shouted Warren, "Go see if you can find some of that gum in Donnie's room!"

"Warren, that was fifteen years ago and there isn't any grape bubblegum in his room now," Janet yelled back in exasperation.

"Well, little fellow, I guess you and I will have to take a walk to the corner store and get some of that gum," shouted Warren.

Andrew stopped his screaming and pounding and took Warren by the hand, using the other arm to wipe away the tears with his pajama sleeve.

"Warren, you can't take the boy to the store in his pajamas," scolded Janet.

"Oh, yes I can!" he retorted as he and Andrew headed for the front door.

****

"Hi, Mom. Where are the kids? Did their mother come get them?" asked Linda as she walked in the kitchen.

"No, I called the phone number the children gave me several times, but I only get an answering machine. They're all out playing in the pool. Your father is watching them."

"You're kidding! Daddy's not sitting in his recliner watching TV?"

"No, he hasn't been in it all day! In fact, he took little Andrew to the corner store this morning to buy him some grape bubblegum."

"Well, well, that's a breakthrough! Maybe you should keep the kids?"

"Linda, please don't call them kids. They are children, not baby goats," her mother gently scolded. "Did you talk to April?"

"No, I keep getting 'the cellular subscriber you are calling is not available," Linda said.

"I can't help getting upset at a mother who would just drop off her children at a stranger's house and leave without even a hello or good-bye," Janet said. "You should see their clothes. They're so worn looking."

"So why don't you take them shopping?"

"That's a great idea. Will you go with me? It's been a long time since I've shopped for little ones."

"Mom, what makes you think I could be of help? I have *never* shopped for little ones. But I'll go. I'm up for a new adventure."

"Good," said her mother. "Can you help me take lunch out to the swimmers?"

Chapter 4

Here We Go, Laughing and Scratching

"I am not going clothes shopping!" said Shawn. "Andrew and I will stay here. Shopping for clothes is for girls."

"My, my, aren't we the macho man," said Linda.

"That's okay," said Warren, "Andrew can take a nap and Shawn and I will be macho. I don't like clothes shopping either."

****

All the girls piled into the car. As Janet was backing the car out of the garage, Kimber said, "Here we go, laughing and scratching."

Surprised, Linda asked, "Laughing and scratching? Where did you get that?!"

"That's what our daddy said whenever we went somewhere in the car," said Dawn.

"This is a nice car and it's really big. Our car is smaller," said Kimber.

"Our car is disgusting," said Dawn. "Very old and ugly. The paint is chipping off, the air conditioner doesn't work, the antenna is broken, the glove-box door doesn't latch, and one of the windows won't roll up unless you pull on it."

"Wow, sounds like my first car Dad bought me at a salvage yard," said Linda.

The children would not tell Janet their last name, so she thought if she could get them to talk about their grandparents it would slip out. "Dawn?" asked Janet, "tell me about your grandparents."

"Our mother's parents were killed in an auto accident when I was six, so I don't remember much about them. About all I remember is that Grandma Georgia would make us apple turnovers for breakfast and Grandpa Jim would put us up on his shoulders and let us touch the ceiling. Mom was sad for a really long time after they died. Dad's parents live in Montana and we haven't seen them very much. Since our Dad's funeral, we haven't seen them at all. They said after their son's death it was too painful to look at his children," said Dawn with a little contempt in her voice.

"It sounds like a lame excuse to me, and who wouldn't want to see their grandchildren—especially these children," thought Janet.

"They do send us nice birthday and Christmas presents," said Dawn.

"Yeah, last Christmas they sent each of us a new winter coat. Shawn got a baseball glove, Dawn got a big book on Australia, Andrew got a fire truck, and I got a baby carriage," said Kimber.

"Kimber, what did you call your father's parents?" asked Janet very sweetly.

"Oh, Grandpa and Grandma Bla…"

Dawn shot Kimber a warning look and put her finger up to her mouth shushing her.

"I can't tell. It's against the rules of The Family Game," said Kimber.

Looking back at the girls, Janet asked, "What family game?"

"Mom!" yelled Linda, "Watch out for that car!" Janet slammed on the brakes stopping just barely before hitting the car in front of her. It took her awhile to calm down and she forgot all about the family game Kimber had mentioned.

Dawn knew it wouldn't be long before Mrs. Chapman would ask about the game again, so she had to think of a way to keep her mind off the game. "The book on Australia was very interesting," said Dawn, "I read it several times."

"She did and she knows all about Australia. Just ask her any question," said Kimber with pride in her voice.

"Okay, what's the capital of Australia?" asked Linda.

"Oh, that's easy. The national capital is Canberra. It's located between Sydney and Melbourne because neither one of the two big cities was willing for the other to win the honor of being the capital."

"That's very impressive, Dawn. You're right!" said Janet.

"Okay, okay," said Linda, "let me ask you another question. What is Australia well known for?"

"Actually there are several things Australia is known for. My favorite happens to be the marsupials, like the kangaroo and koala."

"The wombat and Tasmanian devil are marsupials," Janet replied.

"That's right! There are more than one hundred seventy marsupials whose newborns live in their mothers' pouches for the first four or five months," said Dawn.

"This girl is intelligent," thought Janet, *"but she was not going to let a twelve-year-old outdo her in the knowledge of Australia."* "Captain James Cook discovered Australia in 1770 and charted the whole eastern coast and took possession of it for the British calling it New Wales."

"Mom, I didn't know you knew so much about Australia," said Linda.

"I've read a book or two on Australia in my day."

"You're right about Captain James Cook, but he didn't discover Australia; he rediscovered it," added Dawn. "During the seventeenth century, Portuguese, Dutch, and British navigators carried out preliminary explorations and charted the country's northern and western coastlines."

Linda looked back at Dawn in amazement. "Did you *memorize* the book?"

Janet quickly added, "Did you know that gold was discovered in Australia in 1851 just about the same time gold was discovered in California?"

Dawn gave a puzzled look, "I haven't read about gold being discovered in Australia."

Janet smiled to herself in triumph.

A true competitor, Dawn was not going to let Janet have the last word about Australia. "A prime minister heads the national government," said Dawn. "And there are six states—New South Wales..."

She was going to name all six states, but Janet cut in and said, "Victoria."

Dawn shot back with, "Queensland."

"South Australia," Janet spouted.

Dawn cried, "Western Australia!"

Janet retorted, "Tasmania!" just before Linda said, "Stop, stop! You two sound like dueling Australia encyclopedias!"

****

Warren loved baseball and was so excited when he had a son to share his love of the game. But Donnie only played little league because he could see it made his father happy. Warren was disappointed when Donnie was not very good at the game and he really didn't show much interest in improving no matter how hard Warren tried to teach him. Donnie had other interests at school. He actually preferred to do homework than play baseball. Warren loved his son too much to make him do something he didn't seem to like, so after two years of anguish for both of them, it was decided no more baseball.

While Andrew was down for his nap, Warren and Shawn watched a baseball game on TV and it wasn't very long before Warren had fallen asleep and was snoring very loudly. Shawn decided to take this opportunity to call his mother. To his relief, she answered on the second ring.

"Shawn! I'm so glad to hear from you. Is everything going all right?"

"Yes, Mom. The Chapmans are very good to us. The girls are out shopping and Andrew and Mr. Chapman are taking a nap. Mr. Chapman likes baseball and Mrs. Chapman likes to fuss over us. Andrew follows Mr. Chapman everywhere he goes. I don't think you have to worry about us, so you have a good vacation."

"I'm having a wonderful vacation." Laura boasted. "I'm sitting by the pool and eating nachos. Shawn, I hope all of you are minding your manners and are helping around the house. I don't want Mrs. Chapman to think I didn't teach you anything."

"We are, Mom, but I'd better go before I get caught," he said.

"Shawn, you give hugs and kisses to your sisters and brother."

Rolling his eyes, he replied, "No, Mom. I won't give them hugs and kisses, but I *will* tell them I talked to you. 'Bye." He hung up before she got even mushier.

Laura was so relieved to know things were working out well for her children. Now she could relax while caring for Mrs. Glenn Archer. Her vacation was not a complete vacation, but it was a break from working two jobs. When Mrs. Archer's regular personal assistant took her vacation, Laura took over and stayed with Mrs. Archer. Part of the salary Mrs. Archer gave her paid for the presents her husband's parents sent the children for birthdays and Christmas. She didn't want them to know that their gifts didn't really come from their grandparents. It was more important to her that they felt they were not forgotten.

It wasn't a hard job, but it was confining. For the most part, Laura ate meals with Mrs. Archer at the huge dining table in the formal dining room. They played cards and whenever Mrs. Archer wanted to go out, Laura would go with her. Sometimes Laura would fix snacks when the cooks were off duty. She was able to easily do this in the small kitchen between her modest room and Mrs. Archer's spacious bedroom suite. Her suite was bigger than Laura's whole apartment where she and her children lived.

Bruce and Sally Tyler, the chauffer and his wife, lived over the garage. Brooks Bean was the butler and was in charge of all the household staff. His wife was the head maid and they had nice living quarters in the basement. There were rooms on the third floor of the mansion for other full-time staff, which consisted of three maids and a cook. A part-time cook came in on weekends. There was also a full-time gardener and two part-time gardeners. The head gardener was happy living in a bachelor apartment connected to the building that held all the garden equipment.

Mrs. Bean sometimes would have something for Laura to do, but for the most part Laura took her orders from Mrs. Archer. When Mrs. Archer took her nap, Laura was able to roam the grounds or sit by the pool.

Laura didn't tell the children about Mrs. Archer because it would ruin their fun if they thought she wasn't having a wonderful vacation. When the children asked Laura where she stayed and what it looked like she would describe parts of the Archer's mansion.

The first year she described the grand entryway and the large library. The entryway had a mosaic tile floor with the pattern of a huge, brightly colored peacock with fully extended tail feathers. A huge chandelier with hundreds of crystals and lots of small light bulbs hung above the mosaic peacock. There were four niches on the side-walls, two on either side. Each niche had a very expensive-looking vase placed in it. Beyond the peacock and on the left side were eight-foot tall, solid cherry double doors that led into the library. On the right side beyond the peacock were double French doors that led into an elegant dining room. There were dark cherry-wood antique side tables with matching marble tops on either side of the doors. Fresh flowers from a garden on the grounds were placed at the center of each side table. Also on the side tables were crystal dishes filled with all sorts of candy. She just added that to make the children's mouths water. At the end of the entryway were grand staircases on either side circling up to the second floor, forming a balcony. The stairs had blue carpet that matched one of the blues in the mosaic peacock's tail feathers. The banister and railings were cherry wood polished to perfection. In the center of the two matching curved staircases was an eight-foot statue of a Roman maiden with water coming out of the pitcher she was holding that fell into a round basin circling the statue.

She described the dining room and the grand ballroom the second year. This year she would tell her children about the Roman-style pool and the formal garden with neatly cut hedges that formed a maze.

Chapter 5

Hawaii Shirt

The girls came giggling in through the garage door with pizza boxes and stuff to make a salad. They also had ice cream and root beer.

"It's about time you got home. It's almost 6:30 and we're starved," exclaimed Warren.

"Dinner will be ready soon," said Janet, "Linda, could you make the salad, and Dawn, would you set the table, please?"

"Can we eat outside by the pool?" pleaded Kimber, "I'll help Dawn."

Shawn remembered what his mother said about helping, so he asked if he could bring anything in from the car. It took him three trips to get all the shopping bags into the family room.

****

After everyone had their fill of pizza, salad, and root-beer floats they all went to the family room.

"It looks like Christmas in here," said Warren.

The girls pulled all the stuff out of the bags showing the boys the new things Janet bought them. Everyone got several outfits—pants, shirts, socks, shoes, shorts, and tops. Each girl got a dress with a little purse. Kimber got a new ballerina outfit; Shawn a baseball and glove; and Andrew a Tonka dump truck. Dawn got books and accessories for her hair. Everyone got new swimsuits.

"I hope you like the clothes we bought you, Shawn," Janet said. "Your sisters picked them out. They said you don't much care about what your wear, but they did get you some nice things."

"They're fine, but I really like the baseball and glove. Thank you, Mrs. Chapman."

"Grandpa, we got you a Hawaii shirt and I picked it out myself," Kimber said, as she pulled it out of the bag.

"Those are the biggest, brightest flowers I have ever seen on a shirt. It's very nice, Kimber," Warren grinned.

Janet reminded them, "Time to put all your new things away and think about getting ready for bed."

As the children were gathering up their things, Andrew climbed up on Warren's lap and fell asleep.

"He seems to like your lap, Mr. Chapman," said Shawn, "I'll take him and get him ready for bed."

"Shawn, would you like to go to a baseball game tomorrow?" asked Warren.

"Really? You'll take me to a baseball game?!"

Warren laughingly responded, "I guess that's a yes?"

Dawn slipped beside Shawn in the hallway and whispered, "I need to talk to you tonight."

****

"The children are all down for the night," Janet said as she walked back into the family room.

"Sit down, Janet," said Warren. "We need to talk about these children."

"I know. I don't know what to do. I haven't been able to reach their mother and April is not answering her cell phone. So now I'm worried about April, too."

"I'm sure April is fine. Her cell phone is probably out of range. Remember the same thing happened last year and you worried for nothing." Janet nodded in agreement. "So now what are we going to do about the children?" Warren asked.

"I can't just put them out on the street like their mother did."

"Now, Janet, don't be so hard on her. You don't know the whole story," he said. "Besides, she didn't put them out on the street. She dropped them off at our front door."

"You're right… I have no grounds to judge," she sighed.

Smiling at his wife, Warren said, "That was a very nice thing you did today buying them new clothes. It seemed to make them happy, especially Dawn."

"We had a great time together today. I really like these children."

"I do too," he said, still smiling.

"I assume you know we're going to church tomorrow," said Janet.

"I guessed as much. Can I wear my new Hawaiian shirt?"

"I don't think so." His wife laughed and put her arm around him as they walked down the hall.

Janet went to sleep the minute her head hit the pillow but sleep did not come to Warren. He was concerned about Janet getting too attached to the children who had shown up on their doorstep. Their mother would probably be back sometime and take them away and he didn't want Janet to get her heart broken.

He remembered the first time he saw her at the school district office working as a secretary for the superintendent. She was wearing a yellow dress that highlighted her long, strawberry-blond hair. She was just a tad plump, but it looked good on her. He chuckled to himself at the way she had tried to act so professionally all the time. He would do things to get her flustered but she was one "tough nut" to crack! His company had been hired to design the two new schools in the district. It was going to be a big project—a grammar school, first through eighth grade, and a high school. The two schools would be side-by-side. He was the newest architect with the company so he was the "go-fer boy." He didn't mind because it meant a lot of trips to deliver papers to the superintendent. Sometimes he even made up excuses to go to the district office just to see Janet. She was a bright girl and figured out what he was doing and one day she asked him if he was ever going to ask her out. It was his turn to be flustered, but he got over it quickly. A year later they were married.

****

Shawn fell asleep waiting for the signal that the coast was clear to talk with Dawn. The signal was when he heard Warren snoring. He woke up in the middle of the night and tiptoed into the girl's room. Dawn was sound asleep and Shawn had to shake her several times to wake her. "What is it, Shawn?" Dawn said, perturbed that her brother woke her up.

"You wanted to talk to me, remember?"

"Oh! Yes, I do! What took you so long?" she retorted.

"Mr. Chapman didn't go to sleep right away, and don't talk so loud," he scolded.

"We've been so busy I haven't had one minute alone with you. Have you talked to Mom?" she whispered.

"Yes, I talked to her last night. Now can I go back to bed?"

"What did she say? Is she having fun? Does she miss us?"

"'Yes' to all of those things," he said with impatience. "I'll tell you more in the morning. Now good night." On his way out, he stubbed his toe on something in the darkness. He grabbed his foot hopping on the other foot whispering, "Ow, ow, ouch!"

Dawn put her head under the covers to muffle her giggles.

Chapter 6

The Family Game

One night, two and a half years earlier during their weekly family meeting, the children wanted to know why they never got to see their dad's parents. They asked, "Don't they love us?"

Laura told them, "Of course! They love you very much."

"But they don't even send us presents for our birthdays and Christmas." That's when Laura decided she needed to give the children gifts and put their grandparents' names on them.

"We haven't seen them since Daddy's funeral," they whined.

Laura gave the excuse that Grandpa Blaine was very busy with the big cattle ranch and he probably couldn't leave.

"Then why can't we go see them?" the children asked. Laura told them that she couldn't afford to get them to Montana.

At the next family meeting, the children decided they wanted Laura to call their grandparents and ask them to send the money for airline tickets so all four of them could spend some time on the ranch. "After all, they have a big cattle ranch; they should be able to afford airplane tickets," they said. "We can have a vacation with Grandma and Grandpa and you can have a vacation from us."

"But you already get to stay with your Aunt Jackie," said Laura, reminding them about her sister.

"I know we do," said Dawn, "but we can only go one at a time. We want to all go together, so you can have a break and go on a wonderful vacation."

"What makes you think I want to have a break from you?" Laura asked her children. She said she would think about it and would give them an answer at the next family meeting. She was not about to call her late husband's parents.

After several attempts to get their mother to call the Blaine grandparents, they gave up and Dawn came up with a new plan. She called it the "Adopted Grandparents for a Week Game." It was later shortened to the "The Family Game."

At the weekly family meeting, Dawn presented her plan.

Laura would drop the children off late at night a few houses away from the chosen grandparents' house. The children would dress in their oldest clothes and put on sad faces so they would look pitiful when the grandparents answered the door. The grandparents would feel sorry for them and let them in the house. The children would then tell the grandparents they were supposed to babysit them until their mother came back. Because the grandparents were picked out carefully, they would caringly take the children in while they tried to sort out whether the children's mother had made a mistake and dropped them off at the wrong house. If all went the way the children planned, the grandparents would enjoy having the children around and be like real grandparents. The children would call Laura and report on how things were going and she would make the decision whether or not they could stay. If they were to stay they had to call her every other day. At the end of the week she would pick them up at the same place where she dropped them off. Kimber and Andrew were too young at this point, so only the twins would go the first year.

Laura was stunned but the children thought it was a great idea. Laura could see the excitement in her children's faces and she didn't have the heart to tell them it was the most outlandish idea she had ever heard. Instead she told them there would be too many problems to pull off "The Family Game." They wanted to know what problems there could be. Laura told them the most obvious problem was who would be the adopted grandparents. The children couldn't answer that question but by the next week they had it figured out. They told her *she* could find the grandparents.

"What, me? How am I going to find them?" she gasped.

"You could ask some of your co-workers about their parents. We will even give you all the questions to ask. When someone has all the right answers about their parents, they will be our adopted grandparents."

"I can't do that! People will think I'm too nosy. Besides, even if I do agree to find the grandparents, there are too many other problems." Each week Laura would present a problem to the children and the next week they had figured out a way to solve the problem.

During the next few family meetings they talked about her questions and problems with the plan. Each time, the twins had all the answers...

First, she asked them, "What if the chosen grandparents call the police?"

The twins piped up and said, "If at any time the grandparents act like they are going to call the police, we will leave, call you on a cell phone, and you can come pick us up immediately."

"How can I pick you up immediately if I'm away on vacation?"

Again, the twins had a quick answer. "We'll call Aunt Jackie." Laura smiled to herself, knowing her sister Jackie would tell them how stupid their plan was. But to Laura's horror, Jackie thought it was an ingenious plan and even knew a couple that would be just perfect for the grandparents. They lived two houses away from her and she could keep an eye on the children while they were there.

Next? Laura needed to know who would pay for the cell phones. She certainly didn't have the extra money. The twins said they would earn the money.

Shawn would carry eighty-year-old Edna Stewart's grocery bags from the car into her apartment every Tuesday. She lived in the same apartment complex and very week she tried to pay him and he would never take the money. She always asked him if he was ever going to take the money and he said he would if he needed it. Now he needed it. In fact, he had already asked her if she had any other jobs he could do for her. She told him she was having a difficult time carrying her laundry baskets to the laundry room. He was happy to accept the job and even volunteered his sister to do Mrs. Stewart's laundry. He told her that Dawn does a good job now and doesn't turn his t-shirts pink anymore. Edna chuckled and told him maybe they could work something out.

"What if you lose the phone?" questioned Laura.

"Oh, Mother, we won't lose the phone. Shawn will keep it in his pocket or hidden in his suitcase at all times."

Laura kept thinking of every possible problem she could. She asked, "What if one of you gets sick or breaks a bone and has to be taken to the hospital?"

"Mom, that's easy. The other twin will call Aunt Jackie on the cell phone."

"But where will Kimber and Andrew go while I'm gone?"

Again, Aunt Jackie came to the rescue and had offered to take Kimber. And Mrs. Sanders had already agreed to keep Andrew. Mrs. Sanders cared for Andrew when Laura was at work and while the children were at school. She had a son Andrew's age.

"We'll do yard work for Mrs. Sanders until we've earned enough money to pay for the baby-sitting bill."

Knowing how grandparents like to spoil kids, Laura was concerned about them buying clothes and toys for the children. The twins said they would really try to discourage them from spending money on them. And they would leave anything that *was* bought for them behind so no one would be accused of stealing.

The twins got around their mom's worry about the adopted grandparents calling the police to report her as an unfit mother by promising to never tell their last name, where they lived, or what school they attended.

Laura was beginning to see that the twins seemed to have an answer for everything...

She finally asked, "What if they want to see you again?"

Dawn replied, "Mom, if they don't know where we live or our last name, they won't be able to find us. We'll pick new grandparents the next year. It's pretty simple. Really!"

Knowing her children had thought through everything and were so responsible, Laura finally gave in. Dawn and Shawn drew up a contract with all the rules of The Family Game. They both signed it and even had Aunt Jackie sign the contract. They presented it to their mother to sign. Laura was not happy that her sister had encouraged the twins with this outlandish game. She had secretly hoped something would go wrong with the plan and the children would get discouraged. But that didn't happen. She was now faced with signing the contract or being the villain. She reluctantly signed the contract.

Jackie told Laura, "Don't worry so much; it will be fine. In fact," she told Laura, "my husband, Justin, is Mrs. Glenn Archer's attorney. You know the lady that lives at Heather Glenn? She told him she needed someone to be her personal assistant for a week. She asked him if he knew anyone she could trust and said she would be very generous with the pay. I could suggest you for the job! You can arrange to take a week off from both your jobs and work for Mrs. Archer and make a pot of money. That way the twins will think you are on vacation and you don't even have to leave the city. You know I will keep Kimber that week and Mrs. Sanders has agreed to take care of Andrew."

"Well," Laura said sharply, "you have it all figured out, don't you?"

"Laura," Jackie said with a soothing voice, "you forget your children are not doing this just for themselves, they want you to have a vacation too."

Chapter 7

Baseball Game Monday

Shawn told Warren how his father had taken him to baseball games before he was killed and he had not gone to a game since. Warren was very tender-hearted even though he seemed a bit of a grouch as he grew older. "Shawn, I know going to this game won't be the same as going with your dad, but I'm pleased you want to go with me," he said as he handed Shawn his ticket. Shawn handed his ticket to the ticket collector who scanned it with his hand-held device.

"Young man," said the ticket collector, "this is your lucky day! You are the one millionth fan to enter the Raley's Baseball Park." The River City High School marching band marched towards Shawn and Warren playing "Take Me Out to the Ballgame." Red, white, and blue balloons were released into the air. There was even a local television station filming the event!

A Sacramento newspaper reporter interviewed Shawn and asked him his name, but he only volunteered his first name. When the reporter asked Shawn his last name, Warren's interest perked up. Shawn was silent so the reporter asked again. "Son, I need to know your last name so I can put it in the newspaper."

Shawn looked up at Warren, paused a few seconds, and then said, "My name is Shawn Chapman." Warren smiled at his newly-acquired grandson.

The River Cats' mascot, Dinger, escorted Shawn and Warren to the River Cats' Owner Suite overlooking home plate. Shawn was presented with a River Cats' t-shirt and cap. They were told they could order anything they wanted to eat compliments of the River Cats. They ate while watching the teams come out onto the field to warm up. Before the National Anthem and Pledge of Allegiance, it was announced that this game was dedicated to all the soldiers who had lost their lives serving to protect our freedom. Shawn looked up at Warren and said, "This game is dedicated to my dad."

The newspaper reporter had followed Shawn and Warren into the suite to get more information for his article and overheard Shawn. Shawn placed his hand over his heart and proudly sang the National Anthem and said the words to the Pledge of Allegiance. Warren could not remember when he was more touched by this magnificent tradition to honor The United States of America and what it stands for.

The reporter, eager to learn more about Shawn's father, thought about what a great human-interest story it would make if this young fan was the son of someone who had lost his life for our country. "Shawn?" asked the reporter, "I heard what you said about this game being dedicated to your dad. Was he killed in Iraq?" Shawn nodded his head.

"I'm very sorry to hear that," said the reporter. "Would you mind telling me his rank and name? I want to put it in the article I'm writing."

Shawn didn't know what to do. If he told the reporter his father's name he would be breaking the rules of The Family Game but, on the other hand, he wanted the world to know how proud he was of his father. He looked up at Warren with a pleading 'What should I do?' look. Warren said softly, "It's okay, Shawn. You can tell him."

Shawn said proudly, "My father's name is Christian Blaine. He was a Staff Sergeant in the U.S. Army."

"Thanks, son," said the reporter. "You must miss your father very much. But I'm confused. You told me your last name is Chapman."

Warren came to Shawn's rescue, and said, "I'm his Grandfather Chapman. You can leave out the Chapman and put his name as Shawn Blaine." Shawn smiled at Warren with an expression of gratitude.

The manager of the River Cats asked Shawn if he would like to go sit in the dugout and meet the players. "Oh, boy, would I!" Shawn exclaimed. He then thought to ask Warren if it was okay. Warren smiled at Shawn and nodded his head.

Warren enjoyed watching Shawn having a great time. It was not as good as Shawn being at the baseball game with his father, but it was a close second. And the best was yet to come.

The team gave Shawn a baseball they all signed and a bat that had been used in the warm up. Shawn was taken out onto the field and introduced as the one-millionth fan to attend a River Cats baseball game. It was announced that Shawn's father had been killed in Iraq and how happy the River Cats Association was to present him with season tickets for him and a friend. Then the announcer said those famous words, "Play ball!"

Shawn threw out the first ball to start the game. He pinched himself several times throughout the game to make sure he wasn't dreaming. Best of all, the River Cats won the game.

****

Upon their arrival home, they were met with, "Well, you're finally home!" Janet exclaimed. "I was starting to worry! It's so late."

"The game was tied and they played extra innings." replied Warren.

"Did you have a good time?" Janet asked, even though she could tell from their satisfied grins that they had had a great time. "Dawn made some cookies. Would you like some?" she asked.

"I don't think so," Shawn said, doubting they would be any good. "I'm pretty tired. I think I'll go to bed. Grandpa, thanks for taking me to the baseball game. I had the best time ever."

When Shawn had headed to bed, Janet asked, "He called you Grandpa! What happened to Mr. Chapman?"

"I'll tell you in the morning. I think I will hit the hay, too," said Warren.

"Aren't you going to watch the news?" asked Janet.

"No, I'm too tired and you look like you had a busy day yourself."

"I have," she sighed. "I took Kimber to her ballet lesson, chased Andrew around, and I had to cut another gob of grape bubble gum out of his hair today. Oh, and they *love* the swimming pool. It's hard to keep up with the wet towels! We need to get some new pool toys and maybe you can repair the swing set. Oh, and I also gave the girls a cooking lesson."

As they walked down the hall, Janet put her arm around Warren and said, "That was a nice thing you did, taking Shawn to a baseball game."

"We had a great time together. He's a good boy."

Janet had noticed that Warren was a changed man since the children had been with them. He was happier, his attitude was better, and he didn't sit in that recliner barking at her all day. She had to admit that she also was in a better mood and didn't point out Warren's bad habits as much.

✳✳✳✳✳✳✳✳✳✳✳✳

Early in his career as an up-and-coming architect, Warren had the privilege of knowing where the new schools were going to be built because he was working on those projects. His company was also building a housing project around the schools. He noticed that one of the streets ended where the two schools would share a grassy field. Thinking of the future, he had purchased the lot at the end of that street long before the houses were to be built. After he proposed to Janet, they talked about the house they would build. He wanted Janet to be a partner in designing their new home. They wanted to have three children so the house had to have four bedrooms. They also wanted to have a large kitchen. Janet wanted the children to be able to sit at the kitchen table and do homework while she was cooking dinner. Warren built a chain-link fence between the schoolyard and their side yard. He put in a gate so the children could walk across the field to their school. He didn't want his children walking on the street on the way to school. They planned to put in a swimming pool when the children were old enough to be good swimmers. Their life plan went perfectly and when the children were all in school, Janet applied to work in one of the school offices. She was also a member of the PTA. Warren was a hard worker and sometimes worked long hours, but he always put his family first. In fact, putting his family first got him fired from his job several times, but his boss always hired him right back.

Chapter 8

Super Store

"Warren, I couldn't find the newspaper this morning. I wonder if the paper boy forgot us again today," said Janet.

"No, he didn't forget. I already got it."

"Any interesting news?" asked Janet.

"No, just the same old stuff."

There was an article with a picture of Shawn with his last name in one of the sports pages. Warren made a promise to Shawn he wouldn't not tell Janet his name. He took the sport pages and stashed them away so Janet wouldn't see them.

"You want French toast and sausage for breakfast?" asked Janet.

"French toast and sausage! That sounds yummy," said Shawn. "Better than the cold cereal we have at home."

"My, my, something smells really good," said Linda, as she came into the kitchen.

"How were your flights?" asked her mother. Linda was an airline flight attendant, flying from Sacramento to Dallas and then on to New York for a layover, three times a week. She stayed with her brother, Donnie, when she was in New York.

"The flights were fine except that 'Rico Suave' was on one of them. That's what we've nicknamed him because he thinks he is irresistible to women. He is so obnoxious, always insisting I go out with him. He's like a shark in for the bite and kill. He just won't leave me alone," said Linda with disgust.

Kimber remarked, seriously, "Why don't you 'thumb him on the nose'? That's what you're supposed to do to sharks when they try to bite you."

There was dead silence while everyone looked at Kimber. Janet and Linda were trying not to snicker. They didn't want to hurt Kimber's feelings because she had sounded so completely serious.

"Well, a thumb on the nose sure would have discouraged me. I'm so glad Janet didn't thumb me on the nose when I asked her out," chuckled Warren. That was too much for Janet and Linda and they erupted in laughter.

The children were little chatterboxes while eating breakfast, telling about their fun adventures. Kimber talked about her ballet lesson and how she learned all five ballet positions—both feet and arms. She even got up from the table to demonstrate. Shawn talked about everything that happened at the baseball game, but he didn't tell the part about being interviewed. Dawn talked about the new books she checked out from the library. Among them were cookbooks. Andrew just listened and ate his breakfast.

"Andrew," said Janet, "I haven't heard you say anything this morning. In fact I don't believe I have ever heard you say anything at all! How do you like the French toast?"

Andrew closed his eyes, puckered up his lips, and turned his face away from Janet.

"Andrew doesn't talk," said Dawn. "The doctors say he will talk when he is ready and has something to say".

"Oh, that's right. I remember you telling me that the first night you were here," said Janet.

"I noticed he didn't say anything when we went to the store. I thought he was just bashful," said Warren.

"Oh no, he isn't bashful," said Shawn. "He has his ways of letting you know what he wants."

"Yes, I guess you're right. I've seen his ways," said Warren.

"Oh my, I didn't know it was so late! Kimber, go get your ballet things. I don't want you to be late for your lesson. Dawn, would you get Andrew bathed and dressed and would you also make a list of pool toys you would like to have? Shawn, you and Grandpa can look at the old swing set and decide what needs to be repaired. Linda, would you do the breakfast dishes?"

"Who do you think I am, 'Lindarella'?" said Linda to her mother.

Warren chuckled and said, "Linda, I think you had better do what your mother tells you. I haven't seen her this happy since you and your brother and sister were young!"

After everyone had left to attend to their marching orders, Linda asked her mother, "Are you taking Kimber to ballet lessons every day?"

"Yes, you should see her. She thrives in the classes and it's like looking at you dance when you were her age. She's very good and the teacher said if she had a lesson every day, she could catch up with the other students and be in the beginners' recital."

"Mom, just how long do you think these children are going to stay?"

"I don't know. I can't think about that right now. Come on, Kimber, we have to go."

****

"Warren, where's Linda? I was hoping she would stay home with Andrew while the rest of us went to the Super Store," said Janet.

With a chuckle, Warren replied, "You mean Lindarella? She left after she did the dishes, swept and mopped the floor, cleaned out the fireplace, dusted, vacuumed, and a million other house-cleaning chores."

"Very funny. She would never do all that. Warren, would you mind staying home with Andrew? He will need to take his nap," said Janet.

"I would love to stay home and take a nap myself, but I need to get several parts to repair the swing set."

"Write me a list and I can get them for you," volunteered Janet.

"Janet, I could write you ten lists and draw you pictures but you still wouldn't get the right parts. Andrew and I will have to go to the Super Store with you." Janet knew he was right. As hard as she tried, she could never get parts he needed right.

****

A little bit later, they all piled into the car—three in front and three in back. "Boy, with everyone in here, the car isn't so big—it's jam-packed!" said Kimber.

"It sure is!" said Warren, "I think we need to rent a van to fit everyone. Janet, what do you think?"

"I think it's a good idea. We could get one with a built-in car seat for Andrew." She smiled at Andrew sitting in the back seat between Dawn and Shawn.

"Can we get one with a video player?" asked Kimber.

As Warren backed the car out of the driveway, Shawn, Dawn, Kimber, and even Janet said, "Here we go laughing and scratching!" and they all giggled. On the way to the Super Store the children had fun deciding what accessories they wanted in the rented van.

When they entered the Super Store, Janet said. "We'll probably need two carts."

"Two carts!" exclaimed Warren. "And just how are we going to fit two carts full of stuff in the trunk of the car?"

The children headed for the pool section with Janet, Warren following close behind. Shawn picked out two big water guns. Dawn wanted things that would sink to the bottom of the pool because she liked to dive down to retrieve them. Kimber got four different bright colored, long, spaghetti-looking foam things—pool 'noodles'. Andrew picked out a wind-up motorboat. An assortment of inner tubes, and water wings were also selected.

While the children were looking for more interesting pool toys, Warren told Janet he was going over a couple of aisles to find the parts for the swing set. Andrew followed him and put his arms up to be held. "I can't hold you now. I need to find the parts to fix the swing set, so it will be safe to play on," said Warren. "Go find Shawn to hold you."

When the children were satisfied they had gotten all the pool toys they needed, Janet headed them over to where Warren said he would be. "Warren, where is Andrew? He followed you," Janet said with alarm.

"I don't know. I thought he was with you. He wanted me to pick him up, but I couldn't. I told him to find Shawn. Shawn, did you see him?" asked Warren, trying to stay calm. Shawn shook his head 'no.'

Janet was worried and started barking out orders. "Shawn, you and Dawn go to the toy department to see if he wandered over there. Warren, you look around here to see if maybe he is wandering around looking for you. Kimber and I will go back to the pool section and we'll all meet back here."

They hurried off to their assigned areas to find Andrew. After looking and calling Andrew's name with no luck, Janet spotted a store employee and told him that she could not find her grandson. The employee said he would get the store Security Officer. The rest of the family had come back about the same time the Security Officer arrived, but they didn't have Andrew. Janet asked the Security Officer if he would announce Andrew's description on the store overhead sound system so other customers could help find him. He said he couldn't do that because it was against store policy.

"Store policy!" Janet snapped. "What store policy? My grandson is missing and we need help!"

"Madam," said the Security Officer trying to keep a calm voice, "In one of our other stores, a little girl was lost and her description was announced that if anyone found her to take her to the nearest store employee. A couple did find her and were noticed by a store employee as they were heading out of the store with her. So after that it has been a store policy not to announce lost children."

That bit of information only enhanced Janet's panic.

"Well, do *something.*" Janet demanded.

Warren could see the children were also showing signs of panic in their faces. "Janet, it will be all right. We'll find him," Warren said, trying to be convincing, and putting his arm around her, but he was very concerned himself.

The Security Officer was talking into his radio when there was a very loud earth-shaking scream that came from several aisles away. "I had better go see what that's about," said the Security Officer.

The situation had become too much for Janet and she buried herself in Warren's arms. He took her to a nearby patio chair and gently sat her down. He told the children to stay with her. Janet was beside herself.

"How am I going to tell the children's mother that I have lost her baby son?" she thought.

The girls huddled around her trying to comfort themselves by comforting her.

Warren and Shawn caught up with the Security Officer only to see a woman with a horrified look on her face, pointing to a shelf full of towels. Warren's imagination got the best of him and he thought, "What if someone has hurt Andrew and hid him in the towels?"

The Security Officer reached in and lifted out the little limp body of Andrew. Fear gripped Warren as the Security Officer gave Andrew a gentle nudge in his side. Andrew opened his eyes, put his arms out to Warren and fell back to sleep in Warren's arms.

A crowd had gathered around to see what the scream was all about and their faces all showed relief when they saw that little Andrew was okay.

The lady who screamed said she had reached in to get a couple of towels when she saw the child and it wasn't moving. She thought the child was dead, so she screamed.

Andrew didn't get to sleep long because of all the hugging and kissing he got from his worried family. He didn't even get scolded for the wad of grape bubble gum in his hair. He didn't know why he got so much attention, but he seemed to enjoy it. The little group gathered themselves together, got their carts full of treasures, and headed for the check out, eager to get out of the Super Store.

Chapter 9

Grape Bubble Gum

Janet decided she wanted the children to help out around the house. She was impressed with the way they kept the bedrooms very tidy. She never had to pick up after them. They even brought the towels from swimming into the laundry room.

She gathered the children in the family room and told them. "I was thinking about assigning each one of you extra chores around the house and we would pay you an allowance." She looked at Warren and he smiled in agreement.

"We don't mind doing the extra chores, but you don't have to pay us," said Shawn. "You and Grandpa have done so much for us already we couldn't take any of your money."

"Well, I thought each one of you could buy your mother a little present with the money," said Janet. She thought if she could get the children to discuss what they might buy their mother she could learn

48

more about her. The children didn't talk about their mother and Janet thought it was a little unusual

"That is very nice of you, but our mom wouldn't want us to take any money from you," said Dawn.

"Why don't we assign the extra chores and you can decide later about the allowance. I think it's a good thing for children to have responsibilities," Janet said.

"My mommy says that, too," chirped Kimber.

Janet was having mixed feelings about their mother. She couldn't find fault with the way she was raising her children because they were so polite and helpful. But on the other hand, Janet was still confused with why she just left them on her doorstep.

Janet assigned the three older children extra duties, but Andrew was left out.

"What about Andrew?" said Kimber, "What can he do?"

Janet thought a bit, "Well, if he wouldn't get that grape bubble gum in his hair and leave it everywhere, I would be happy. I found two pieces of chewed gum by the edge of the swimming pool melting in the sun. I stepped on one of them and spent some time getting it off the bottom of my shoe. I guess he leaves it there because he can't chew gum and swim at the same time." Janet sounded a little more critical than she intended, and she felt bad as soon as the words came out of her mouth. Andrew jumped off of his chair and ran down the hall toward the bedroom he slept in.

"Oh, now, Janet, you've hurt his feelings," said Warren. "I'll go see if he's all right."

But before he could get up out of the chair, Andrew was back. He had one hand behind his back and with his other hand he took out the gum he was chewing and handed it to Janet. He then drew out the hand from behind his back and handed her the rest of the new gum. He smiled up at her and she knew what he meant.

****

While Kimber was dusting the table in the entryway, she found an envelope that had fallen down behind the table. The Chapman name and address was written in fancy writing.

Mr. and Mrs. Warren Chapman and Family. The sender's name was *Mrs. Glenn Archer, Heather Glenn Estate.*

"What's this, Grandma?" asked Kimber holding out the envelope to Janet.

"I forgot all about that. Open it up and read it," said Janet. Dawn stopped the vacuum when she saw Kimber open the envelope. Kimber handed the envelope to Dawn to read.

Mrs. Glenn Archer requests the presence of

Mr. and Mrs. Warren Chapman & family

to join her at Heather Glenn Estate
& for a black-tie dinner party.

August 23, at 6 p.m.
Mrs. Archer will send a car
to pick you up at 5:30 p.m.

Dawn's excitement got the best of her and uncharacteristically, she blurted out, "Can we go?"

"Go where?" asked Warren, as he walked in through the patio door.

"To Mrs. Archer's yearly dinner party," said Janet.

"Oh, we can't go this year. We have the children and it would be a long, boring night for them," Warren grinned with relief.

"Why can't we go? We've always taken our children in the past."

"Grandpa, we want to go," Kimber pleaded.

Dawn had regained her composure. "We drive by Heather Glenn Estate on our way to school and have always wanted to see what was behind those huge iron gates."

"Then it's settled; we're going. I'll call Mrs. Archer and tell her we will be there with four grandchildren."

Kimber ran out the patio door to tell Shawn. He was cutting the grass when he saw her running towards him, both arms waving over her head and her mouth flapping. He thought she looked quite comical because he couldn't hear her over the mower. She reached him and yelled in his ear, "We're going to Heather Glenn Estate."

"Weather what state?" he yelled back.

"No! *Heather Glenn Estate*; the big house," she shouted.

"What did you say about the big mouse?" he shouted back, teasing her now. She put her hands on her hips, made a face in frustration, and walked away.

After the children finished their chores, they went swimming. Warren and Janet sat drinking lemonade and watching the children play with the new pool toys. Andrew was learning to swim around with the water wings and become brave enough to venture away from the side of the pool. Janet watched him very closely because she didn't want another big scare with him. Shawn had great fun with the giant squirt gun. He would squirt one of the beach balls to see how fast he could scoot it across the pool. He liked to upset Dawn by shooting at the neighbor's cat when it sat up on the fence. Dawn was good at diving down and retrieving the objects that sank to the bottom of the pool. Kimber was happy floating around on the noodle foam pretending she was a synchronized swimmer. They discovered if they filled the hollow center of the noodle with water and blew on one end a stream of water came out the other end.

"It's nice to sit here and watch the children get some use out of the pool," said Warren with a sigh.

"What are we going to do when their mother gets back from her vacation and claims them? It will leave a big hole in our lives," Janet said sadly. "Kimber said they're playing a family game, but every time I quiz them about it, they find a way to change the subject."

"Janet, you mean to tell me you let them get the best of you? That's not like you."

"I know, but I think if I find out what the game is, they'll go away. I don't want them to go away."

"I didn't see Andrew smile very much at first; but he smiles a lot now. Especially the big smile I got when he gave me his grape bubble gum. I worry about him not talking, but he sure has warmed up to you, Warren. He follows you everywhere you go."

"It might be because he hasn't had a father or grandfathers around to spoil him," said Warren.

Kimber got out of the pool and trotted over to Janet, shivering. Janet wrapped a towel around her and started to rub her vigorously with it to warm her.

"What does 'black tie' mean?" Kimber asked.

"It means you have to dress in a monkey suit," said Warren, smiling.

"You mean we all have to wear money suits—like Halloween?"

"No, Kimber," said Janet. "Your grandfather is just teasing you. It is a slang word for a black suit and black bow tie."

"Do Shawn and Andrew need to wear a black suit and bow tie? Because they don't have one," Kimber replied.

"Oh, my, you're right! And you girls will each need a dressy dress." Janet jumped up and called to the children. "Get out of the pool now; we need to go shopping."

"Now?" asked Warren.

"Yes, we only have a few days and the boys suits will need to be fitted."

The children all piled out of the pool and Shawn was walking beside Warren.

"You know I don't like to go shopping," Shawn complained to Warren.

"I don't either, but it will make you grandmother happy so it's something we need to do. This time you'll have to bite the bullet."

****

Mrs. Archer's personal assistant called and wanted to know if she could have another week of vacation. Her sister had become ill and was in the hospital. She wanted to stay with her. Under the circumstances Mrs. Archer felt she had no choice but to grant the extra week. She asked Laura if it was possible for her to stay another week. Laura said no at first because she spent her second week of vacation with the children. It was the highlight of the year and she didn't want to miss it.

Laura was concerned because it had been more than two days since she last heard from the children. She knew it was risky but she decided she had to call them. She waited until 2 a.m. because she didn't want the Chapmans to know she was calling. She also hoped that Shawn kept the cell phone close by him so the ring would not wake anyone else. He answered on the fifth ring. "Hello," he said in a sleepy voice.

"Why haven't you called me?" his mother demanded. "It's been over two days. The rules of the game are that you call me every other day."

"I'm sorry, Mom," answered Shawn, more awake now. "We've been so busy and having so much fun I forgot to call."

"You know the week is up this Friday night," his mother said.

"Already?" he questioned.

"You must be having a good time at the Chapmans."

"We are, Mom. It's so cool here. Grandpa is taking me to a baseball game Friday night and I don't want to miss it. Can we stay a little longer?" he pleaded. Laura didn't answer right away. "Mom, are you still there?"

"Yes, I'm here. Don't you miss me?" she asked.

"Of course we miss you, Mom, but we're having such a good time and that's what you wanted. Are you having a good time?"

"I would if I didn't miss my babies so much," she gushed. Shawn hated it when she called them her babies and she knew it.

"Mom, we are not babies. Can we stay a little longer?" he pleaded again.

"Okay, you can stay another week," she said.

"That's great, Mom. Thank you. Grandpa and I can go to more baseball games." He was wide awake now.

Chapter 10

Surprise Encounter

"Janet, the car is here," called Warren. He and the boys were all ready and waiting for the girls. Kimber led the parade, her sister next, then followed by Janet. The girls had matching light blue, princess-style taffeta dresses with crystal beading around the slightly scooped neck and hem of the capped sleeves. Kimber had blue socks that matched her dress and white patent leather Mary Jane shoes. Dawn had nylons and one-inch heel white pumps. They each had their hair pulled back at the sides and ringlets hanging down their backs with several matching long thin blue ribbons tied around the barrette that held their hair. Janet had a darker blue crepe floor-length dress. It had a sequin and pearl short-waist jacket.

Warren thought his wife looked beautiful and told her so. He told the girls they looked like beautiful little princesses. The truth is they looked like they were going to be in a wedding.

When Janet saw Shawn dressed in his black suit with his curly hair cut shorter, she was taken back to someone she hadn't thought of for a very long time. Warren wore the same black dress suit he had worn every year with a bow tie. The little well-dressed group climbed into the waiting limousine.

"Where are the seat belts?" asked Kimber.

"Some limousines don't have seat belts," said Warren. Free from a seat belt, Andrew started to jump up and down on one of the crushed velvet seats waving his arms around.

"I guess that's why it's called a monkey suit," Kimber joked.

Everyone laughed as Warren grabbed Andrew and pulled him onto his lap. "Okay, little monkey, it's time to act like a well-behaved little man."

****

Laura was propped up on her bed, finishing the last chapter of a book when she heard the buzzer sound in her room. That was the signal from Mrs. Archer when she wanted Laura's assistance.

Mrs. Archer had several maids hovered around her helping her get ready for the dinner party when Laura arrived. "Oh, Laura," said Mrs. Archer, "you won't need to join me for dinner tonight. I'm having a dinner party for one of my husband's associates and his family. Why don't you take the evening off? Maybe you'd like to see a movie? Grace, would you go fetch the newspaper and bring it to Mrs. Blaine?"

"Yes, madam," Grace said as she curtsied.

"I just love it when they curtsy," beamed Mrs. Archer. "Thank you for staying another week, Laura."

Laura didn't find a movie that interested her so she decided to go down to the library and look for another book to read.

****

The children caught their breath as the limousine drove through the huge open iron gates to the mansion. They had always wanted to get a better look at what was beyond them. Now they were actually driving through them in a limousine! They looked out the windows as the limousine drove up a long, tree-lined driveway that led to a house bigger than they had imagined. The butler and a maid were waiting for them as the limousine pulled up in front of wide circular stairs that lead to the entry. The porch had two large urns containing curly Cypress trees on either side of the tall, double-front doors. The driver opened the door and assisted each passenger out of the limousine. The butler greeted them and led them into the grand entry, the maid following behind.

Kimber held out a small lavender suitcase to the butler. He raised his eyebrows with a questioning look. "It's my ballet costume," explained Kimber. Without expression he took the suitcase and handed it to the maid.

Laura was deep in concentration looking for an interesting book when she heard footsteps on the entry tile floor coming toward the library. Not wanting to be seen, she ducked behind one of the large, overstuffed sofas just as the butler led the guests into the library. "You may wait here," said the butler. "Mrs. Archer will be down shortly." Laura could hear the sounds of people sitting down on the large sofas.

The children's eyes were wide as they looked around the massive room. The back wall was completely covered with shelves crammed with books. On the wall to the left of the bookshelves was a huge fireplace. It was so big you could have fit a small table and chairs in it to eat lunch. Over the fireplace was a giant tapestry of a hunting scene with a small fox followed by hound dogs and people on horseback all dressed up with funny hats. On either side of the fireplace were floor-to-ceiling windows with heavy burgundy drapes. A burgundy wingback chair with ottoman was facing the fireplace and a round dark wood table was beside the chair. It had a lamp with a gold shade trimmed with gold fringe around the bottom.

On the other side of the chair was a stand that had holes in it with a different shaped pipe in each hole. On either side of the fireplace standing in front of the heavy burgundy drapes were tall suits of armor with headgear and jousting sticks. On the other side of the room, in the corner opposite the bookshelves, was a large round table with twelve chairs placed around it. On the wall above the table was a picture of King Arthur and the Knights of the Round Table seated at a table identical to the one in the room. The wall opposite the fireplace had four tall French doors with the same heavy burgundy drapes, but they didn't entirely cover the doors, so you could see out onto a courtyard. In the middle of the room were three large over-stuffed burgundy sofas arranged in a U shape. There was a square dark wood coffee table with large carved round legs. On top of the coffee table were several oversized books of old castles and King Author and the Knights of the Round Table.

"Mrs. Archer must be very old to have read all these books," said Kimber. Laura's ears perked up—that little voice sounded just like her Kimber's voice.

"I don't think she read all the books herself. Maybe Mr. Archer read some of them. Can I go look at the books?" Dawn asked, looking at Janet. Now Laura was on alert because *that* voice was definitely Dawn's.

"I don't think so," said Janet. "Maybe we should wait for Mrs. Archer and ask her."

Andrew slipped off the sofa and ran behind it. He stopped dead in his tracks when he saw his mother crouched down on the floor.

Laura stared at her little son dressed in short black pants with suspenders, white shirt, and a black bow tie, knee-high black socks, and the cutest little black loafers. His hair had been cut short and no longer looked chopped from having grape bubble gum cut out of it.

He looked so adorable it took all her will power not to gobble him up into her arms. She put her finger to her mouth in a shushing motion and moved her head back and forth. As much as she wanted Andrew to start talking, she hoped this would not be the time.

"Andrew," called Janet, "come back here and sit on Grandpa's lap." Andrew scampered back to Warren who lifted him onto his lap.

Laura closed her eyes and gave a silent sigh of relief. She couldn't help but notice that the older couple had been accepted by her children, and they had been adopted as grandchildren. She thought that she should be pleased to know her children were being treated with kindness, but what she felt was a strong case of jealousy.

Mrs. Archer entered the library in grand fashion. "It's so nice to see you again, Janet, and you, too, Warren." Mrs. Archer extended her hand to them. "These must be the grandchildren you spoke of. How did you acquire four beautiful grandchildren since last year?"

"It's a long story," said Janet.

"Well, you can tell me over refreshments," said Mrs. Archer. Warren introduced each of the children to Mrs. Archer and Kimber gave a polite curtsey, because she thought Mrs. Archer looked just like a queen. The curtsey pleased Mrs. Archer and she took Kimber's hand and said, "Come along, Kimber, you can help me lead the guests to the east sitting room. I don't much care for this room. It was Mr. Archer's room. He let me design and decorate the house except for this room. He wanted a part of the house to look like the inside of a castle. It's between an old English hunting lodge and King Arthur's castle. He sat by the fireplace and smoked those ghastly pipes. The room is too dark and gloomy for my taste."

Laura waited until she thought the little group would be walking out the library doors. She slowly lifted her head up to catch a glimpse of her children. She only saw their backs but they looked like little angels. She had not talked to them for several days and she missed them so very much. Andrew turned back and saw his mother's head peeking over the sofa and gave a little wave. When they were all out of sight, Laura crept over to the double French doors that led out to the courtyard. She walked down the wide steps through the rose garden and made her way to the back of the mansion. She entered the door where deliveries were made. Inside the door was an entry hall that had a butler's office to the right. To the left of the entry was a large door leading into a kitchen that looked like it belonged in a large restaurant. At the end of the entry hall was a staircase leading up to the small kitchen between her room and Mrs. Archer's bedroom suite.

Laura flopped down on the bed thinking about what she had just seen. It was wonderful to see her children, but now she wanted to get a better look at them. Maybe if she peeked through the windows that looked into the east sitting room she could see them. No…that wouldn't work. The drapes would be closed to block the heat of the day. She would have to wait until they got into the dining room to get a peek. Across from her room she could look over the banister and see the library doors. So she thought if she walked to the other staircase, maybe she could see the dining room doors. Laura opened her bedroom door, checked to see if anyone was around, and walked past Mrs. Archer's master suite to the other staircase.

She was pleased when she could see the dining room, but she discovered she had to lie down and peek through the banister spindles to be able to get a good view of the dining table. As she was assessing the situation, the dinner party guests came into view so she had to scoot back to duck out of sight. Laura waited for them to go into the dining room. But to her surprise, they started up the staircase just below her! Laura backed up as far as she could against the wall trying to keep out of sight. She felt behind her for the utility closet doorknob so she could slip into the closet. But to her relief, they only went up a few stairs to get into position to pose for a picture. When Mr. Archer was alive, he hired a professional photographer from one of the most popular studios to take pictures of the invited families and Mrs. Archer had continued the tradition.

After waiting what seemed like an eternity to Laura, the guests headed for the dining room and settled into their chairs. She slithered down and again strained to see between the spindles of the banister. She watched each one of her children separately. Shawn sat tall and looked older dressed in his black suit. Tears filled her eyes; he looked so like his father. His twin sister looked angelic and lady-like. Kimber was very animated and seemed to be doing most of the talking. Then there was Andrew. He was just plain adorable and even seemed to be smiling a little. She was pleased to see that they were using the proper table etiquette she had taught them.

She thought about how each week she taught them a new skill and they had the whole week to practice. The child that remembered to model the skills most properly got a special treat at the end of the week. She usually figured out a way to give each child a treat. Laura was so engrossed with watching her children she didn't hear Mrs. Bean walk up behind her.

"Mrs. Blaine, what on earth are you doing down there?" demanded Mrs. Bean.

Startled, Laura hit her head on the banister rail as she jumped up.

"Are you alright?" Mrs. Bean asked with a stern, puzzled look on her face.

Rubbing her head, Laura stammered, "I'm fine." She hurried off to her room, closed the door behind her, and flopped down on the bed. She was disappointed she didn't get more time to watch her children; they looked so happy. How could they be so happy without her?

"*Now stop that. I'm just being selfish. After all, they are playing this game for me so I could have a nice vacation,*" Laura thought. She sat up and then the thought came to her; "*What a sight it must have been for Mrs. Bean to see me spread out on the floor with my head almost glued to the banister.*"

Laura started to giggle and giggle and then she couldn't stop giggling. But the giggles turned into sobs. She didn't want to be here. She wanted to be home with her children.

There was a knock on the door from the small kitchen. "Mrs. Blaine, are you in there? I've brought your dinner." Laura held her breath to control the sobbing, and managed to say, "Leave it on the counter, please."

Chapter 11

The Dinner Party

"Shawn," asked Mrs. Archer, "What is it that you like to do?"

Washing down a mouth full of garlic mashed potatoes with milk, he said. "I like baseball. Grandpa and I have season tickets for the River Cats games. We've gone twice and both times the River Cats won."

Mrs. Archer smiled with approval. "When Mr. Archer was alive he took me to several River Cats games. We had a company suite and he would invite some of his favorite employees to the games. Warren, if I remember right, didn't you and Janet go on several occasions?"

"You're right," said Warren. "Glenn and I both loved baseball."

"When Glenn was a young man he would go to the Sacramento Solons games at Edmond Field on Broadway and Riverside. It's been torn down and now a discount store is on the property. Warren, do you remember the Solons?" asked Mrs. Archer.

"Yes, my dad took me to games every season as a birthday present, starting when I was seven years old. Joe Marty was my favorite player; he played outfield and he was a great hitter. I collected baseball cards," said Warren as he reminisced.

Out of the corner of her eye, Mrs. Archer could see that Andrew had finished eating, and was now squirming in his chair and pulling at his bow tie. "Andrew," said Mrs. Archer, "It looks like you did a fine job eating you dinner. I must compliment you on your good behavior, but I bet you've had enough of sitting still. Would you like to go play in the game room where there are lots of fun toys? Would that be all right, Janet?"

Janet nodded her head 'yes' and said, "That would be fine."

"Brooks, would you take Master Andrew to the game room?" Brooks walked over to Andrew, put his large hands under Andrew's armpits, and lifted him up out of the chair holding him at arm's length, pivoting around like a robot and placing Andrew gently on the floor.

"Brooks, do try to smile. You will frighten the boy. Have Mrs. Bean look after him," said Mrs. Archer.

"Yes, Madam. Come along, Master Andrew," said Brooks as he forced a reluctant smile.

Kimber put her hand over her mouth and tried to stifle a giggle. "Is Mrs. Bean's first name Lima?" she asked, trying not to laugh.

Mrs. Archer answered with a smile, "Yes. As a matter of fact it is!" And everyone at the table erupted in laughter.

Andrew followed along after Brooks trying to keep up. Mrs. Bean was not very happy about watching Andrew. In fact, the very words she spoke to her husband were, "What does she think I am? A nurse-maid?" Andrew's eyes lit up when Mrs. Bean led him into the large game room filled with more toys than Andrew had ever seen in one place.

****

Laura just picked at her food. She could only think of her children down in the dining room. She decided to take the dinner tray down to the kitchen herself. Maybe the kitchen staff might be talking about the dinner guests. She was not disappointed. There was talk about how well behaved and what good table manners the young guests displayed and how adorable the little boy looked when Mrs. Bean took him to the game room. The staff giggled when they heard that Mrs. Bean didn't look very happy about it.

Laura could not resist. She went to the game room to see her baby boy. As Laura entered the room she saw Andrew playing with the toys scattered all around him and Mrs. Bean sitting in the corner as if she was being punished. "Mrs. Bean, if you like, I can look after him," said Laura.

"Oh, that would be great. I'm not very good with children," replied Mrs. Bean.

Andrew heard his mother's voice and jumped up and ran to her with outstretched arms. Laura kneeled down and was almost pushed backwards when he hit. "My, he sure must like you," said Mrs. Bean. She didn't give it another thought. She was happy to be relieved of childcare duties.

****

"Kimber," Mrs. Archer asked. "What would you like to be when you are older?"

"I want to be a ballerina. In fact, I'm taking ballet lessons every day," beamed Kimber.

"You know, I thought you were a ballerina by your curtsey and the way you walk," said Mrs. Archer.

"What do you mean by 'the way I walk'?" asked Kimber with delight.

"Well, ballerinas walk a certain way and that's the way you walk."

Kimber's face beamed with pleasure and she said, "I'm going to be in a ballet recital Saturday night. Would you like to come?"

"Oh, I would love to, but I'm having another dinner party that night."

Kimber looked disappointed but then she remembered. "Oh, I can dance for you tonight because I brought my ballet costume!"

"I think that would be wonderful" said Mrs. Archer.

Brooks had just walked back into the room. "Brooks, see that the dance studio is readied for a ballet recital."

Brooks rolled his eyes and said, "Yes, Madam," as he disappeared from the room.

Mrs. Archer turned her attention to Dawn. "Dawn, what is your favorite way to spend your time?"

"I like to read," Dawn answered.

"Oh, that's a wonderful habit to have; I bet you're a good student?"

"She is!" piped Kimber. "She gets straight A's and helps me with my schoolwork."

Mrs. Archer smiled with admiration. "I'm so glad to hear you're a good student, Dawn. I guess you noticed all the books in the library. Glenn and I have collected books from all over the world. I bet we have a book on just about every subject you can think of."

Dawn asked, with a touch of uncontrollable excitement. "Do you have any books on near-death experiences?"

"I have several books on the subject. In fact, the reason you are here tonight is because of a near-death experience," said Mrs. Archer.

Dawn's eyes opened wide with interest. She had never heard a personal experience like this before.

Mrs. Archer saw the interested expression on Dawn's face and decided to ask the guests if they would like to hear the story. Before anyone could say anything, Dawn said a bit louder than she expected, "I do!" A little embarrassed by her outburst, she blushed and sat back into her chair. Shawn rolled his eyes and gave that "oh, brother" look, but before he could say anything, Warren shot him a 'don't open your mouth' look."

Mrs. Archer was pleased that someone wanted to hear the story.

Chapter 12

The Story

"My husband, Glenn, wanted three things out of life. He wanted to be powerful, make lots of money, and live in a very large house. He was willing to do whatever it took to achieve his goals. He worked himself to the fullest leaving very little time for anything else. He expected his employees to work just as hard, and if he thought one of them was not working up to his expectations, Glenn would fire that person."

Warren smiled and said, "Glenn fired me several times in the thirty years I worked for him."

Mrs. Archer also smiled, "I always knew when Glenn fired you because he would be in the most horrible mood when he got home. I would ask him, 'Did you fire Warren today?' He would bark back, 'That darn Warren. Why does he make me fire him? He's the best architect in my company.' He would stomp off and yell at any household staff that was in his path. I would have the cook make his favorite dinner and that improved his mood at least a little.

"After a fitful night's sleep, he always called you early the next morning and demanded that you come back to work. Unfortunately, the company lost some very good employees that could not deal with Glenn's explosive personality. Most of them did not come back, and some of them just quit because he was so demanding," sighed Mrs. Archer. "But you always came back, Warren."

"I understood Glenn's desire to build a successful and prosperous company, but I did not always agree with his leadership tactics," said Warren. "When he fired me, I knew he didn't mean it and I would have been back at work the next day even if he hadn't called me. My family was always happy when I got fired because they knew there would be a very generous bonus in my next paycheck. That was Glenn's way of apologizing and I understood that."

Mrs. Archer nodded in agreement and continued her story. "Anyway, all that work, anger, stress, and responsibility of running a large architectural firm caught up with him." She paused a little before going on. "One morning on his way to get into the limousine, he collapsed and fell to the ground, grabbing his chest as he moaned. Luckily, we had two part-time gardeners who were trained paramedics. They saw Glenn collapse, immediately diagnosed that he was having a heart attack, and administered CPR. It was ten minutes before Life Flight landed on the south lawn. If the two paramedics had not given Glenn CPR within five minutes, he would have been brain dead. If the brain is deprived of oxygen for over five minutes, it starts to die. It took another ten minutes for Life Flight to get him to the hospital emergency room. Glenn's heart had not beaten for over twenty minutes. The hospital emergency room doctors worked on him and were able to get his heart started.

"You know, we have one of the top-ranking cardiology hospitals in the nation. Another lucky break was that one of the best heart surgeons in the world was conducting training for the very heart surgery that Glenn needed, so he agreed to do the surgery as a training exercise. Glenn survived the surgery. In fact, the surgeon said it was the best work he had ever done. Glenn's surgery was videoed and has been shown all over the world at hospitals as a training tool. Glenn's recovery was very slow and he was not the same man after his heart attack and surgery. He would sit for hours and stare out the window and not say a word. He didn't even ask about how the firm was doing. The only thing he said about work was 'Put Warren Chapman in charge. He can make all the decisions' and then he never said other word about the work for the next six months." Mrs. Archer had to stop and gain her composure. "Warren, I'm so thankful for you," she finally managed to say.

"That was the hardest six months of my life," said Warren. "I had a better appreciation for Glenn's hard work."

"It was a hard time for me, too," said Mrs. Archer. "The hospital director put a small bed in Glenn's private room for me to sleep on. His room was in the Jim Hudson wing of the hospital. The wing was named after my father because he donated a large amount of money to help build it. I rarely left Glenn's side and fed him most of his meals. He was never a very affectionate man and sometimes I wondered if he ever really loved me. But during those long days and nights in the hospital, I realized just how much I cared for and needed him."

Mrs. Archer had to swallow hard to hold in her emotions. "I was so exhausted when he was finally released to come home. He had twenty-four-hour nursing care so I was able to get some rest, but I still kept a close eye on him. One morning when we were having breakfast, he looked at me with such love in his eyes. I was stunned. With a gentle voice he said, 'I want to name our estate Heather Glenn.' I looked at him puzzled because I didn't know what he meant. He told me he wanted everyone to know that I was first in his life and he counted himself as second.

This time Mrs. Archer was unable to hold back the tears and had to stop to compose herself. "As I told you," she finally continued, "Glenn was never very affectionate and it was very awkward for him to express endearing words. I knew putting me first was a monumental change in his mindset." She again stopped and dabbed at her face with her napkin. "Before, he always considered himself first above anyone else.

"'Heather,'" he said again with the same gentle voice as before. "My heart jumped because I knew something profound was coming. He told me he knew he had died and would not be here today if it had not been for some very miraculous coincidences.

"I told him I knew we were very lucky. He looked at me with moistened eyes and said. 'It was not luck, it was a blessing.' Glenn told me while he was dead it was shown to him that he had not been a very nice man. And most of all, he had been a very difficult person to live with. He felt all the hurt he caused the people around him and he was aware of all the time I stayed with him at the hospital and wondered why I would do that, especially after the way he had treated me throughout our marriage. He said, 'If things had been reversed and you were the one that had the heart attack, I would not have done the same for you. I know now it was because, for some reason, you really cared for me and... will you forgive me?'"

The tears were running down Janet's face. Warren reached under the table and took hold of her hand. Dawn and Kimber were also crying. Shawn wasn't really sure how to handle so much emotion and wished he was with Andrew.

Mrs. Archer had stopped again to take a sip of water to stifle her emotions. "Glenn told me," she continued, "that he was given a second chance to make things right and needed to make up for so much. In the past, he had been intolerable with the household staff. He would yell at them for no reason and always find fault with their work. He would tell me, 'You need to intimidate them to keep them on their toes.' It was so hard to keep a full staff of servants. The word got around about Glenn, and the agency I used would not send any more people over. I think I went through about six agencies. Finally, I made a deal with one agency to send over extra people to do a good cleaning while Glenn was on his monthly trips to check up on the satellite offices.

Brooks and Lima Bean were the only ones loyal to us. Brooks' father had worked as a butler to my father and Lima's mother was my mother's personal maid. Oh, yes," Mrs. Archer chuckled, "the cook, Gertrude, was not intimidated by Glenn. If he came into 'her kitchen,' as she called it, she would chase him out with the frying pan saying things in German I didn't understand! He fired her so many times I lost count. She was like you Warren—she never left."

"Well, I guess I'm getting off the subject," said Mrs. Archer. "Where was I?"

"Mr. Archer needed to make up for his bad deeds," answered Dawn.

"Oh, yes. Glenn went on to say that he wanted to have a Christmas party for all the staff, their children, and their grandchildren. He wanted to give each family member $100 so they could buy something nice to wear because he was going to have family portraits taken. He told me to hire temporary staff to do all the preparations so our regular staff wouldn't have to prepare for their own party. He asked me to hire a personal shopper to buy each one of them a very nice Christmas present. In addition, he was going to give each staff member a $1000 bonus. He said money wouldn't buy their friendship. He knew he had to earn that, but it might make their lives easier for now.

"He had been a beast to all the people that worked for him and he needed to do something about it. He knew he couldn't make it up to the employees he fired unfairly or the ones that left because of him. But he was going to have a big family picnic here at Heather Glenn for the ones who still worked for him. He had been planning everything in his head the last few months and he knew just what he wanted.

"I tell you, my head was spinning with all these declarations Glenn was making. I said to myself, '*Who are you and what have you done with Glenn Archer?'* Janet, do you remember that first year and how crowded it was here at Heather Glenn with all the families?"

"Yes, I do! It was crazy, but our children talked about it for weeks. Glenn had planned so much entertainment for the children that the parents just sat back and visited with one another. I think the first year was the best," said Janet.

Mrs. Archer continued, "As it turned out, Glenn decided Heather Glenn was not big enough to handle all the families, so the following years he bought a whole day at the water park for the family picnic.

"But he wasn't done. He had one more thing he wanted to do. He wanted to invite each one of the architects who worked for him and their families to a formal dinner party—the ones here in town could come to Heather Glenn and for the employees that work at our satellite offices, we would travel to them. 'We will have a family dinner party at the best hotel and each family will stay in a suite for the night,' he said. He wanted to know them personally and learn the names of their children and what they like to do. He also wanted this to be an annual event so he could continue to learn about the families.

"We were unable to have children and Glenn would never agree to adoption. After his near-death experience, we were too old to adopt children of our own, so he made the household staff and his firm's families our children. Glenn lived for another ten years, but he asked me to keep up the tradition of the formal dinner parties after he died. So that is how a near-death experience brought you here."

"It's like the Scrooge story," said Kimber.

"You're right, Kimber, it does sound like the Scrooge story," agreed Mrs. Archer. "Now let's go see your dance recital."

Chapter 13

Déjà Vu

Mr. Archer had had the billiard room converted into a large play-room for children when they visited. There was a large custom-made carpet painted to look like a town. It had roads, a river with bridges, a neighborhood with houses, a fire station, police station, hospital, church, and other buildings with Heather Glenn in the middle of the town. There were vehicles made especially for the carpet. Andrew took the fire engine and placed it at the fire station. He handed his mother a limousine and she placed it at Heather Glenn. They took turns placing all the vehicles were they belonged. The last two cars were a high-way-patrol car and a small red convertible. Andrew handed his moth-er the convertible and he grabbed the patrol car. Laura grinned and sped her car past Andrew's patrol car. He caught on and started his car after hers. She was on her hands and knees crawling around the little town as fast as she could go, running the little red convertible around the roads on the carpet. He was in the patrol car in fast pursuit after her red convertible. Although he didn't talk, he made the sound effects of a police siren. She went as long as she could go before her knees started to burn. She stopped and Andrew ran into her. They toppled over onto the floor laughing with delight. This was the first time Laura had played like this with Andrew. Both she and Christian had played with the other children when they were young but by the time Andrew came along his father was gone and she was a single mother with four children. There was always some chore or something that needed to be done and she didn't have the time to play with Andrew.

Andrew headed for the three rocking horses. The three horses were different sizes, named Baby Bear, Mama Bear, and Papa Bear. Andrew got on Baby Bear and Laura got on Papa Bear and they rocked until Andrew grew tired of it. On another wall were five arcade games that Andrew went to next. They threw balls into three different sized rings and when the ball went into the smallest ring, lights flashed and a buzzer sounded. After they played all the arcade games, Andrew headed for the oversized Lincoln Logs and together they built a very impressive log cabin. To Laura's relief, after that they sat awhile and admired their work, Andrew took her hand and led her to a rocking chair. He went to the bookshelf, grabbed as many children's books as his little arms could carry, and climbed on his mother's lap. She read to him until he fell asleep. The next thing she knew someone was nudging her shoulder and calling her name.

"Mrs. Blaine, wake up," said Brooks. "The guests are leaving and I need to take Andrew." He looked down at the sleeping boy and must have been touched by Andrew's angelic sleeping face because this time he picked him up with more affection. Andrew did not stir, even when Brooks handed him over to Warren.

Mrs. Archer said her farewells to her dinner guests and thanked Kimber for the delightful dance recital. Kimber did a little ballerina curtsey as a 'thank you' back. The driver held the limousine door open while the weary guests climbed in and got comfortable. Warren was still holding the sleeping Andrew. Kimber laid her head on Janet's lap, and the twins sat at the other end of the limousine.

"Did you find something strange tonight?" Dawn whispered to Shawn, trying not to disturb the others.

"You mean that strange near-death experience story Mrs. Archer told?" he answered.

"No, something else," said Dawn. "Besides, that was not a strange story; it was a wonderful story."

"It was a mushy story. Mrs. Archer cried the whole time," Shawn replied.

Dawn didn't want to pursue the discussion any further because she wanted to talk to him about something else. "The peacock. Didn't the peacock look familiar to you?"

"The peacock? What are you talking about?"

"The entryway—the whole entryway. I think I've seen it before," she said. "Same thing with the library—the gold carpet and the hunting tapestry over the fireplace mantel. I think I have seen that before, too."

Shawn gave his sister his 'look' and said, "Maybe you saw it in a magazine?"

"No, I didn't see it in a magazine. Didn't *anything* look familiar to you?" she asked again. He didn't answer because as much as he wanted to deny it…he also had a vague feeling that the house seemed familiar.

"It's like déjà vu," Dawn said.

"Deja what?" Shawn asked.

"Déjà vu—like you have lived through the same moment before," she explained.

"Well, maybe the house is haunted and Mr. Archer is still lurking around," Shawn snickered.

Dawn was so exasperated at her brother that she huffed and folded her arms over her chest. She pushed her head hard against the plush upholstery of the limousine and closed her eyes thinking about the things she had seen at Heather Glenn. She had never been to Heather Glenn; so why was she feeling she had been there before? Then it hit her. Her mother! It was her mother who described the things which she had seen. Her eyes flew open, and she leaned over to Shawn and said, "It was Mom!"

Shawn had already stopped thinking about Heather Glenn and was thinking about the next time Grandpa and he would be going to another baseball game. "What?" he said. "What about Mom?"

"Remember when she came back from her vacations she would describe the places where she stayed?"

"Yeah, a little," Shawn answered. "I wasn't much interested in all that stuff."

"Well, for example the entryway. She described the mosaic peacock on the floor and the double circular staircases and the rest of the things in the entryway—even the flowers on the side tables," said Dawn.

"No," said Shawn. "She said there were bowls filled with candy on the side tables and I didn't see any candy tonight."

"So you did listen," Dawn smiled. "How about the library? She described that, too. The big burgundy couches and the suits of armor. Do you remember that?"

"Yeah, I suppose I do," he painfully admitted.

"How do you explain that Mom described the rooms at Heather Glenn?" she asked her brother.

"I don't know," he said. "You're the one who figures everything out. Maybe Mrs. Archer went to the same places on vacation that Mom went and she liked it so much she made her house look the same." He smiled because he was pleased with himself. He had come up with a great explanation. Usually it was Dawn who had all the smart ideas.

"I suppose it's possible, but really? What are the odds?" she asked.

The limousine came to a stop and the driver opened the passenger door. The others had all dozed off on the plushy, cozy, smooth ride home and had not heard the twins' interesting conversation.

"Grandpa?" asked Shawn as they were getting out of the limousine, "Did you believe that story Mrs. Archer told about her husband's near-death experience?"

"Shawn, I saw a very work-driven man who did anything to get what he wanted. He was short tempered, intimidating, and cared little for others feelings. Whatever happened in those twenty minutes when his heart stopped beating changed him. He was the opposite of his former self, just as Mrs. Archer said in her story."

"Dawn" asked Kimber in a sleepy voice, "Was I ever at Heather Glenn when I was little and don't remember? Because I remember that big blue peacock on the floor."

"No, you've never been there, but I also remember the big blue peacock and other things too."

Chapter 14

The Auto Circle

The next day, after breakfast had been devoured, Warren announced that they were all going to the Auto Circle to check out a van. "I called George who worked with me at the Archer Architectural Firm. Mr. Archer fired him and now he works at one of the auto dealerships selling cars."

After Mr. Archer had the heart attack, he went to see George and apologized to him for the way he had fired him. George accepted the apology and told Mr. Archer that as it turned out, he was better at selling cars than as an architect and had worked his way up to fleet manager. Mr. Archer bought two brand new cars from George and gave them to the wives of the two paramedics who saved his life.

"George is going to help us find a van so we won't be like sardines when we drive around."

"What should I wear?" Dawn asked Janet. She wanted to make sure she dressed right for the occasion.

"Well, it's kind of tricky what you wear to buy a car. You don't want to overdress because they'll think you have lots of money and won't be willing to bargain for the price of the car. But on the other hand, you don't want to dress too casual because they'll think you can't afford a good car and will show you only junky ones."

"We aren't going to buy a van—just rent one," Warren said. "I'm going to wear the Hawaiian shirt Kimber picked out for me," he teased Janet.

Janet didn't pay any attention to her husband, "So," continued Janet, "I'm going to wear slacks and a silk blouse. Why don't you wear your jeans and that pretty pink silk top? That way we will look stylish yet casual."

****

Warren pulled into the Auto Circle. There were dealerships on both sides of the street. "Do you know exactly where the dealership is?" asked Janet

"No" answered Warren.

"Maybe you should get into the middle lane," suggested Janet, "so you could go either way."

"What's the name of place we're looking for?" asked Shawn.

"It is called 'Deal Dealership'," answered Warren.

"There it is on the right, Grandpa," said Shawn.

"Get over in the right lane, Warren," spouted Janet, "or you'll pass it up."

"I can't. There's a car on the right of us."

"Slow down and let him pass," ordered Janet. Warren was slowing down but the car on his right slowed down too.

"Grandpa, you passed it up," said Shawn.

"I know," Warren shot back. "That imbecile next to us slowed down."

"Warren! The children," Janet warned.

"They're probably looking for a dealership, too," said Dawn.

"Just make a U-turn and go back," said Janet.

"I can't. This is a one-way street. That's why it's called it the Auto Circle because it goes around-and-around one way in a circle. I'll have to go all around the circle again to get there."

"Warren you had better get in the right lane so you won't miss it again," warned Janet.

"I know," said Warren sounding a little irritated. "I know what I'm doing. Please just let me do the driving."

It was silent in the car until Warren pulled into the Deal Dealership. Everyone piled out and walked into the showroom. Janet and the children looked at the brand new minivan while Warren asked the receptionist to page George.

"I like the blue color," said Kimber.

"I like the leather seats," said Dawn.

Shawn was not interested in the minivan and headed for the black convertible sports car. He climbed into the driver's seat and started to examine the dashboard instruments. Andrew followed his brother and pulled on Shawn's shirt motioning that he wanted to sit on Shawn's lap. "So you like this car, too," said Shawn, as he lifted his little brother onto his lap. Shawn grabbed the steering wheel and pretended that he was driving in a race. Andrew mimicked his brother and grabbed the middle of the steering wheel where the horn was. The horn was very loud and echoed through the showroom. Andrew jumped and let go of the steering wheel. But when he noticed that everyone in the showroom was looking over at the black convertible sports car to see who had honked the horn, he grinned with glee and grabbed the horn again. This time he did not let go and the deafening honk bellowed through the showroom, the sound bouncing off the windows and the hard surface of the tile floor. Salesmen and customers were covering their ears and glaring at the two boys in the black sports car. Shawn tried to pull Andrew's hands off the horn but Andrew had a tight grip and wouldn't let go.

George had answered the page and was with Warren as both of them ran over to the black sports car. Warren shouted, "Let go of the horn, Andrew!" Shawn finally pried Andrew's little hands off the horn. The piercing horn stopped just before Warren said "Andrew!" so it sounded very loud and sharp. Andrew looked up at Warren with a frightened look on his face and put his arms out to Warren to get reassurance that he was not in trouble. Warren took Andrew in his arms and said, "Sometimes, Andrew, you try my patience, but I still love you." Andrew put his little arms around Warren's neck and hugged him.

"Well, Warren, what do you think about this sweet SUV?" asked George.

"Does it have a DVD player?" Kimber wanted to know.

"Well, yes it does; it's just hidden." George turned on the engine and with a push of a button the screen came down from above between the two front bucket seats. George slipped in a DVD of cartoons for the children to watch while George showed Janet and Warren the SUV.

Warren was very impressed, "Is this the van we can rent?"

"No, this one you will have to buy," said George.

Warren looked at the price. "This price is outrageous!"

"Well, Warren, when was the last time you shopped for a car? Prices have gone up since you bought that old family car of yours."

"I'll tell you right now I'm never going to pay that price for a van."

"It's an 'SUV'," corrected George. "It just so happens I have a slightly used one parked right out the door."

Warren stuck his head into the new SUV and told the children this was not the van they were going to rent. George was going to show them a used one.

As George walked out the door with the car shoppers, Kimber asked "Does the used van have a DVD player too?"

George said, "Yes, it does. In fact, it has a built-in restraining seat for 'you-know-who,'" as he looked at Andrew.

The SUV had already been started with the A/C running. George opened the passenger door for Janet to get in. "Feel how cool it is inside. This SUV has great A/C and feel that soft leather upholstery," oozed George. "It will clean up very nice after the children." George walked around and got in the driver's seat and pushed a button that automatically opened the two back sliding doors. The children climbed into the SUV to settle in. "Hey, little guy, there's a special seat just for you. Now you can see out the window," smiled George.

"Where's the TV?" asked Kimber? "You said it had a TV." George pulled the small TV screen down from a compartment attached to the ceiling. "It's very small," said Kimber.

George ignored her and showed Shawn the remote for the DVD player and did a quick demonstration. He showed the girls all the cup holders. "How do you like all the space in there? Lots more room than that family sedan."

He got out and motioned for Warren to get in the driver's seat. "Well, there you go, Warren, all set for a test drive." Just as George told Warren not to turn off the engine because it would not start again due to the security system, Shawn pushed the volume button on the DVD player and out blasted *Rugrats*. "Warren, did you get all that about the security system?" asked George.

"Sure, we'll be fine," said Warren.

"Well, do you have any questions about any of the controls?" asked George.

"Nope," said Warren. "I'll figure it out myself. Here we go laughing and scratching!" The rest of the family chimed in with him and they all laughed their way out of the dealership onto the Auto Circle.

"I think I'll take this bucket of bolts on the freeway and see what it can do," chuckled Warren.

"Warren, don't scare the children," said Janet.

"You mean don't scare *you*," answered Warren with a smile. "How's the TV doing back there?"

Shawn was not interested in the *Rugrats*, so he looked out the window and watched the car dealerships pass by, one after another. "I guess you could buy any car ever made here. It goes on forever," said Shawn.

Chapter 15

The Ice Cream Shed

"Oh, look, Warren, there's the Ice Cream Shed! My buddy, Betty, said they make the best ice cream," said Janet.

"Anyone for ice cream?" asked Warren.

They all piled out of the SUV and lined up for an ice cream treat.

"Kimber, what kind of ice cream do you want?" asked Janet.

"I want rainbow sherbet, please," she responded.

Andrew searched back and forth looking through the glass case that held the ice cream, pushing people out of his way until he found bubblegum ice cream and then wildly pointed at it. Shawn got rocky road; Janet and Dawn wanted strawberry; and Warren decided on vanilla.

As the little group sat at a table eating their ice cream, Dawn said, "I read in a book that you can tell someone's personality by the ice cream they like. For example, rocky road was the fourth flavor made after vanilla, chocolate, and strawberry. So, Shawn is an adventurer with a rocky life ahead of him."

"There you go again with your crazy ideas," Shawn said, dismissing Dawn's idea.

"Tell me about my personality?" Kimber asked.

"You are an artist with fanciful dreams," answered Dawn.

"What does fanciful mean?" asked Kimber.

"It means you are like Tinker Bell," said Dawn.

"Oh, good, I like Tinker Bell. What about Andrew?" Kimber asked.

"Andrew is a big bubble getting bigger and bigger and when he pops and starts talking we will not be able to shut him up. As for me," Dawn said, "I'm original, intelligent, competitive, and pleasing to look at."

"Oh, you forgot conceited," Shawn quickly retorted.

"I think she's quite right about herself. That also describes me," Janet said with a playful smile.

"What about Grandpa?" Shawn asked.

"Let me think…vanilla." Dawn paused with a mischievous smile, and said, "Boring." The little group all erupted into laughter. Even Andrew got the joke.

****

"Warren, get the van started. It's hot in here," ordered Janet.

"It won't start."

"Are you doing it right?" said Janet with impatience.

"Of course I'm doing it right. I've been starting cars for fifty years. I should know how to start a car. You put the key in and turn," barked Warren. He was getting hot, too. "It just doesn't do anything—not even any noise. Janet, where's the cell phone?"

Janet started looking in her purse for the phone but she couldn't find it.

"Dump your purse upside down, Janet, and find that phone!" Warren barked again.

"No. I'm not going to empty my purse. I looked and it's not in there," she snapped back at her husband.

"Grandpa," said Dawn "I think you put the cell phone in your pocket when we left home."

Warren felt his pocket. "You're right, I have it," Warren said sheepishly. "I'm sorry for yelling at you, Janet. Let's take the children back into the Ice Cream Shed so they can stay cool and I'll call George."

While Warren was calling, one of the Ice Cream Shed employees asked Janet, "Are you test-driving a car?"

"Yes, how did you know?" asked Janet.

"Because I saw that the SUV wouldn't start. It happens all the time. People see the famous Ice Cream Shed and stop while test-driving a car and forget that the car won't start back up because of the security system."

In the meantime, Warren had gotten in touch with George. "Warren, didn't you remember when I told you the SUV wouldn't start back up if you turned the key off?" George asked with a little chuckle.

"No, George, you didn't tell me the van wouldn't start back up," snapped Warren.

"Well, never mind. I'll come and start it," George said with a calming voice.

✴✴✴✴✴✴✴✴✴✴✴✴

"How come the van wouldn't start?" Kimber asked when George arrived.

"Well, you need to have the 'magic key' to start the SUV," said George with emphasis on *SUV*.

"Why didn't you give us the magic key?" asked Kimber.

"Well, I guess I must have made a mistake and forgot," George said apologetically.

"Well, I guess you did!" said Warren.

George just smiled and said, "Well, how did you all like the SUV?"

"Oh, we like it!" said Kimber, answering for the rest of them.

"Okay, Warren, follow me back to the dealership and we can write up the sale," coached George.

"I'm not going to buy the van. I just want to rent it," said Warren.

"Well, Warren, you and I have been friends for a long time, so I can trust you. Why don't you take the SUV home for a couple of days and see how you like it."

"Can we, please?" pleaded Kimber. "We can take it to Apple Hill so we won't be smashed like sardines."

"Here's the 'magic key', Warren. I'll see you in a couple of days." George quickly walked away and was in his car driving off before Warren could refuse.

Chapter 16

Apple Hill

Dawn and Kimber were doing the breakfast dishes while Janet made the sandwiches for the picnic.

"What kind of sandwiches are you making, Grandma?" asked Kimber.

"They are cheddar cheese, pimentos, and mayonnaise."

"I never had that kind of sandwich before," said Kimber.

"It's what my mother always made when we went on a picnic, so I made the same sandwiches when Grandpa and I took our children on picnics. It's a tradition with our family," said Janet.

"I don't think our family has any traditions," said Kimber.

"Yes, we do," Dawn said. "You just don't remember. What about the times we go visit Daddy's grave every year on our birthdays."

"I forgot about that one," Kimber said, a little embarrassed.

"That's a wonderful tradition," said Janet, as she put a jar of big dill pickles in the picnic basket.

"Are the dill pickles part of your mother's tradition, too?" asked Kimber.

"No, our daughter, April, loves dill pickles so we added them to the tradition. And of course, you can't go on a picnic without potato chips," said Janet.

"Can we add root beer to the tradition?" asked Kimber.

"I think that's a wonderful idea!" said Janet.

"What's going on in here?" Linda asked, as she strolled into the kitchen.

"We're going to Apple Hill," answered her mother. "You look tired."

"I'm very tired. I took an extra shift and just flew in from Dallas. I'm going straight to bed so I'm glad you are taking the kids to Apple Hill for the day. Who's big ugly van is that in the driveway?"

"Your dad is renting a bigger car to drive the children around."

"Okay, okay, but just how long do you think these kids are going to be here?"

"Dawn, would you and Kimber go see if Andrew is ready to go?" asked Janet.

After the children had left, Janet turned to her daughter. "Linda, you didn't need to say that in front of the children. You'll upset them."

"Upset the children? You're upsetting *me*. You and Daddy are spending so much money on children you don't even know. That's just crazy."

"Remember, it was your idea that we take them shopping and you said maybe we should keep the children," answered Janet.

"That was just some clothes because they looked like poor little orphans and it was the charitable thing to do. I didn't think you wanted to keep the kids forever. Oh, and by the way, that nosey Mrs. Grandstaff wants to know where the kids came from."

"You didn't tell her did you? Her husband works for Social Services and it would be just like her to have him send the police."

"What's going on in here?" asked Warren.

"Dad, tell me you are not going to buy the big ugly van," Linda spouted at her dad.

"It's an SUV, and no, I'm just renting it," he shot back.

"Good, good," Linda said as she stormed out of the kitchen.

****

"Okay, are we all settled in with our seat belts on?" asked Warren. "Let's go through the checklist. Picnic basket," Warren said in military style.

"Check," said Janet.

"Ice chest," he said. But there was silence.

"Warren," Janet said, leaning over and whispering in his ear. "That's you."

"Oh, ice chest," he said again and answered, "Check!" There were some soft giggles from the back seat.

"Blankets," he said.

"Check," answered Shawn.

"Paper goods," Warren said.

"Check," said Dawn.

"Good. I guess we're ready to go," Warren said.

"Wait a minute!" wailed Kimber. "What about me? I have the shopping list."

Warren looked at Janet and said to her out of the corner of his mouth. "You didn't tell me about the shopping list."

"Sorry," Janet said looking guilty.

"Shopping list," he said, with more importance then the last time.

"Check!" said Kimber as if it was the most important thing in her life.

"Shawn, do you have the movie ready to start?"

"Yes," he answered back.

"Okay," said Warren. "Here we go." And the rest of them chimed in "laughing and scratching."

"Did you see that, Janet? That guy turned left on a red light. It was blatantly red because I have the green light. I should have run him down. The stupid idiot."

"Warren, be mindful of the children," Janet scolded him.

"My daddy used to say that 'Big Uid in the Sky' would get him," said Dawn.

"Who is the 'Big Uid in the Sky'?" Warren asked.

Shawn interrupted his sister. "He's a big hand that comes down out of the sky and picks up cars driven by stupid idiots. Then he spins them around with his finger on his other hand and puts the car down going the opposite direction than the stupid idiot who was driving."

"Of course! With all that spinning, he doesn't know which way he is going!" Warren said with delight. "I like that idea."

The picnickers all traveled in silence in the big cozy van. "It sure is quiet with the children watching the movie," said Warren. "Not like it was with our children arguing, hitting, crying, and constantly asking, 'Are we there yet?'"

Suddenly, Kimber piped up, "Are we almost there yet? I have to go to the little girl's room."

Warren and Janet smiled together. "See, just like old times. Kimber, it's the next turn-off," answered Warren. "We'll stop at the first apple store."

"How many apple stores are there?" asked Dawn.

"There are lots of them," answered Janet. "Too many to see in one day. We will stop at a few of our favorites."

"When are we going to eat?" asked Shawn, "I'm hungry."

"Didn't those six big pancakes fill you up?" teased Warren.

"They did for a little while," said Shawn, "but I'm hungry again."

"They have the best apple turnovers at the first apple store," said Janet.

Warren bought Shawn and himself an apple turnover. "Warren," said Janet, "you're going to spoil your lunch. You're not a growing boy like Shawn."

"I just didn't want him to be embarrassed eating alone, so I got one for myself. Do you want a bite?" asked Warren.

Janet took a big healthy bite out of Warren's turnover and smiled at him. "Shawn, you'd better take your brother to the bathroom," she said. "I'll hold your turnover."

"No, I don't think so, but thanks anyway," said Shawn. "I saw the big bite you took out of Grandpa's," he teased Grandma.

As she started looking around, Janet asked, "Where *is* Andrew?"

"I think he's with Dawn," answered Shawn.

"No, Dawn went with Kimber," said Janet, with concern in her voice.

"Okay," said Warren, "spread out. Janet you check with the girls and Shawn and I will look around the shop." Just as they were ready to spread out, Andrew came walking up, eating an apple.

"Andrew, where did you get that apple?" asked Janet. He pointed over at a big basket filled to the brim with apples. "Andrew you can't just pick up an apple and eat it! You have to pay for it first. Besides, it probably hasn't been washed," she said.

"Oh, I assure you, Madame, that all our apples are washed and very clean before we put them out," said a man standing behind them. "Young man, this handsome lady is right. It is customary to buy the apple before eating the apple."

"I don't think he knows what the word customary means," said Dawn. She and Kimber arrived just as the man made his comment to Andrew. "And I don't think he knows you have to pay first. He never goes to the grocery store with our mother."

"Can I have an apple thingy like Shawn?" asked Kimber.

"Young lady, that is called an apple turnover," said the man.

"Okay, I want one, please," said Kimber.

"I tell you what. Why don't you two young ladies split one? It's on me," the man said. "But, young man, you must pay for your apple," he looked directly at Andrew.

"I wonder if he is related to Brooks?" Shawn mused. "He sure sounds like him."

Warren gave Andrew some money to pay for the apple and the girls thanked the man several times for the turnover before they left.

Chapter 17

Diversion

"The next apple store is a gift shop," said Janet. "You can find a special gift for your mother if you'd like." As they approached the store she said. "Warren, you make sure you keep a close eye on Andrew. I don't want him to get into any mischief."

In the store was every kind of thing you could imagine made to look like apples or had apples painted on it. The girls headed for the kitchen supply area. The boys headed for the back yard area. "Have you ever seen anything like this?" said Warren.

"I don't think I have, Grandpa," answered Shawn. They were looking at a huge BBQ shaped like a red apple. "Look, there's a tabletop painted to look like an apple." Andrew ran over to a little chair his size and sat in it. The seat was shaped like an apple and the back was a stem with two apple leaves. "You know, Grandpa, we want to get Grandma a gift. Do you see anything here she might like?"

"Not in this area. I'm the one that does the outdoor cooking."

"Look there's a smoker in the shape of an apple to match the BBQ," said Shawn. "My father used to BBQ when he was alive."

"Does your mother BBQ now?" asked Warren.

"No, not any more. It makes her cry because it reminds her of our dad," said Shawn sadly.

The girls were looking at all the kitchen apple-themed stuff. Janet questioned them on what their mother might like and the girls were questioning Janet on what she liked. They told Janet that if she liked something, they knew their mother would like it. Janet found several things she liked and the girls picked out an item to buy for their mom. Janet went with Kimber to pay for the gift. Dawn found the boys and told them they found something they wanted to buy for Grandma. "Grandpa, can you stage a diversion to get Grandma's attention so we can buy her gift? We want to surprise her."

"I don't think *I* can, but there is a master at staging diversions," he replied, pointing at Andrew.

"Andrew, do you know what a diversion is?" Dawn asked. Andrew shook his head 'no.' "Okay, listen to me, Andrew. We want you to do something to get Grandma's attention so we can buy her a gift." A big smile appeared on Andrew's face.

"I think that's a 'yes,'" said Warren. Andrew dashed off.

"Wait, Andrew," said Shawn as he caught him by the shirt. "You have to wait for the signal. When we tell you to *go*, that will be the signal. Shawn held Andrew's hand to make sure he didn't start the diversion too soon.

"That was a good interception, Shawn," said Janet, as she and Kimber joined the group. "No doubt he was up to some mischief." She gave Andrew a little smile. "Shawn, did you find a gift for your mother?"

"No, not yet."

"Come with me over to the kitchen supplies. There are several things I think she might like,"

"Oh, great," said Dawn, "that's just where we wanted to go."

"I guess we have no choice," said Warren. "Okay, Andrew, time for your diversion." Andrew was off and headed for an apple barrel filled with tennis balls that were painted to look like apples. He picked up as many as he could carry and headed for Janet and Shawn. First he threw a ball at Shawn and then one at Janet and hit her in the back.

She turned around and saw Andrew. "What are you *doing*?" Andrew ran off and stopped when he saw another customer and threw a ball at him and hit him in the back.

"Andrew!" yelled Janet. "Stop that! You're going to hurt someone or break something." Janet stopped to apologize to the customer. Andrew had run out of balls and was headed for the tennis-ball apple barrel. By the time Janet caught up with him he was scooping up apple balls by the arm full and dropping them on the floor. The balls were bouncing every which way. "Andrew!" she yelled at him again, "You stop that right this minute!"

Warren was standing behind a large quilt that was made from all different kinds of fabric with apple prints. He was just out of Janet's sight. He couldn't help himself; he was chuckling at Andrew's antics. He could see the girls in action and when he thought they were close to finishing their task he came out from behind the quilt trying to look serious and scooped Andrew up into his arms. "Okay, Andrew," he whispered in his ear, "that's a good job." Andrew was so pleased with himself that he threw his arms around Warren's neck and gave him a big kiss on his bristled cheek.

"Andrew," Janet said sternly, "Don't think you can hide behind your grandfather's affections. You've made a mess and you need to get down here right now and put the balls back into the barrel."

"Okay, little guy, part of the diversion is to clean up," he whispered into Andrew's ear as he sat him down on the floor. It took Warren,

Janet, Shawn, and Andrew several minutes to get all the balls back into the barrel. The customer Andrew hit in the back even came over to help.

Janet again apologized to him. He said, "It's okay. It didn't hurt; it just startled me. Actually, I remember doing the same thing when I was a little boy and my mother spanked me pretty good."

"Maybe that's what Andrew needs—a good spanking," she said looking sternly at Andrew. Andrew hid behind Warren's legs away from Janet.

"Oh, Janet," said Warren, "don't be so hard on the him. He's just being adventurous."

Chapter 18

TV Stars

"Oh, look, Grandma, there's the TV booth over there," said Kimber.

"I see it. They're giving away fans and it is starting to get hot," said Janet. The family walked over to the table where a familiar looking lady was handing out the fans. Janet whispered into Warren's ear, "I think she's Susan, the one that does the weather."

The lady handed each of the girls a fan. But when she tried to give Shawn a fan, he said, "No, thanks, I don't want a fan. Fans are for girls."

Warren reached out, took the fan, and said, "This is a manly-looking fan. Look, it has the TV station call letters in bold letters and there is nothing sissy about the logo."

The lady laughed and said, "I've never heard our fans called 'manly' before."

"Are you Susan, the weather lady?" Kimber asked.

"Yes, I am. Stick around because I'm going to do the noon weather report live from here. In fact, I need a family for my introduction. Would your family like to be on TV?"

"I would," said Kimber.

Janet gave a doubtful look. "I don't think so. I've already been embarrassed once today."

"Come on, Grandma, it'll be fun," begged Kimber.

"It's very easy," Susan replied. "I'll just ask you a few question on what you like about Apple Hill. It will only take a few seconds."

"We'll do it," said Warren.

Susan got the family in position while the cameraman adjusted his camera. "Okay, Susan, five seconds," said a woman with headphones standing beside the cameraman. She started to count the seconds off with her fingers and pointed to Susan to start.

"Good afternoon. I'm Susan Felt, live from Apple Hill. With me today is the Chapman family. What do you like the best so far at Apple Hill?" She put the microphone in front of Shawn's face.

"I like the apple turnovers," he managed to say.

"How about you, little guy?" She put the mic in front of Andrew. Andrew closed his eyes, puckered up his lips, and hid his face in Warren's neck.

Warren replied for Andrew, "I think he liked the apple tennis balls."

Kimber tugged on Susan's hand, pulled the microphone to her face, and said, "How about me? Aren't you going to ask me what I like?"

The lady that did the count down earlier had both of her hands held up in front of her and mouthed "Five seconds."

Susan said, "Well, there you have it—another happy family enjoying their time at Apple Hill. The weather forecast is next." She waited for the red light to go out on the camera and turned to the Chapmans and said, "You did a great job. Thanks."

✳✳✳✳✳✳✳✳✳✳✳✳

That same day, Mrs. Archer was thinking about where she and Laura would have their lunch. She thought about her favorite place to eat lunch under the quaking aspen trees at the back of the property. She reminisced back when she and Glenn would have lunch there together when he wasn't busy working.

She told Laura, "He liked to sit and look back at the spacious house and landscaping he had created and built. I always felt bad when the staff had to haul the table, chairs, linens, dishes, and food all the way out to the back of the property.

"After his heart attack, Glenn and I spent a lot of time under the quaking aspen trees. He had a golf cart modified with a little flatbed on the back so it was easier for the staff to transport everything.

"One day, we were sitting under the tree listening to the breeze blowing through the aspen trees. The birds were singing and the squirrels were chasing each other in the branches of the trees. Glenn told me that when his time came he wanted to be sitting under these trees right here next to me.

"The next week was Glenn's birthday and I had a special lunch set up for him. I laid out cream-colored linen slacks and a cream silk shirt for him to wear. I wore a cream-on-cream print flowing cotton dress. All the table linens were white to match the white covers on the chairs. The dish chargers and flatware were gold plated. The serving dishes were crystal to match the crystal stemware. The place-settings were cream with gold trim. A crystal vase filled with white daisies was in the center of the table. I had the cook make one of Glenn's favorite lunches and had lemon cheesecake flown in from New York. After lunch, we sat there enjoying the perfect day. The sky was clear blue except for a few puffy white clouds. There was a soft refreshing delta breeze. One of the staff members said that we looked like we were in a perfect movie set.

"Glenn reached over and took my hand and, in a loving voice, said, 'Heather, thank you for this wonderful lunch. It's so peaceful here.' He was smiling at me and never looked so content. 'I'm so happy being here with you. I love you very much.' He was still smiling when he closed his eyes. His head slumped forward.

"Glenn! Glenn!" I called to him. "But he didn't move. I could see he wasn't breathing anymore. Tears filled my eyes and ran down my face. I felt a gentle pressure on my shoulder as though Glenn had put his hand there. I could hear his voice coming from deep inside me, 'It's okay, sweetheart. I'll be waiting for you.'"

Heather dabbed the tears from her face, brought herself back to the present, and thought it was too hot to have lunch outside, so they decided to have lunch in the north sitting room where it was cooler. There was a TV in the room and Heather liked to watch the noon news while eating lunch.

"Oh, look, Laura, there are the Chapmans with those wonderful children. They were here for a dinner party."

Laura snapped her head up to see her children on the TV just as Susan was talking to Shawn. She watched, thinking how comfortable her children looked with the Chapmans. She should have been happy for her children, but she was jealous. She said under her breath, "I should be there with my children, not the Chapmans."

"What did you say, dear?" asked Mrs. Archer.

"Oh, nothing," snapped Laura.

Mrs. Archer was a little surprised at Laura's sharp reply, but she decided to ignore it and try to continue on with conversation. "Janet Chapman told me the most disturbing story on how she became care-taker of those children. She told me the mother just dropped them off at her doorstep and left. What kind of mother would do that?"

"Maybe you haven't heard the whole story," snapped Laura again. Laura was sorry as soon as the words came out of her mouth. She saw the hurt look on Mrs. Archer face. "I'm so sorry, Mrs. Archer. I was way out of line. You have treated me with so much kindness and I had no right to snap at you. I haven't felt very well today. Do you think I could be excused?"

Mrs. Archer's face softened, relieved to know there was a reason for Laura's outburst. "Yes, dear. You should go lie down and rest. I will have one of the staff look in on you later."

"Thank you, Mrs. Archer," Laura said sweetly trying to make up for her earlier outburst.

✳✳✳✳✳✳✳✳✳✳✳✳

"This is the last shop before we eat," said Janet. "Warren, will you and Shawn stay outside with Andrew? I don't think I can go through another one of his adventures. Can you and the boys set up the picnic lunch, please?"

The girls went into the shop with Kimber proudly holding the list in her hand. Janet's neighbors knew she was going to Apple Hill, so they all put in their requests for delicious apple products.

Chapter 19

Applesauce

The children were eager to get back into the van so they could finish the movie they had been watching on the way to Apple Hill. They were half-way home when Kimber said, "Grandpa, the TV went blank."

"Do you know what happened, Shawn?" asked Warren.

"No, the remote control doesn't work."

"I can't look at it right now," said Warren. "I guess we'll have to resort to the old-fashioned way and play a road trip game. It's called 'If Who Married Whom.' For example, if Mary married Mr. Christmas, her name would be Mary Christmas."

"I've never heard of any one with the last name of Christmas," said Dawn.

"I've got one," said Shawn. "If April married Mr. May, her name would be April May."

"No," said Dawn. "If April's middle name was May and she married Mr. June her name would be April May June!"

Shawn glared at his sister and under his breath but loud enough for her to hear, "You always have to outdo me."

"Do you have one, Kimber?" asked Janet.

"I'm still thinking," she answered.

"I have one," said Warren. "If Ima married Mr. Okay she would be called Ima Okay."

The children looked puzzled and Kimber said, "I don't get it."

Warren explained, "Before April had a cell phone and was on her vacation, she called collect and gave her name as 'Ima Okay'. That way we knew she was okay and we didn't accept the collect call, so we didn't have to pay for the call."

"Isn't that cheating the phone company out of money?" asked Dawn, innocently.

"I guess you're right; it isn't very honest," he agreed.

"I have one now," said Kimber. "If Maple married Mr. Tree she would be called Maple Tree."

"Who ever heard of a girl named Maple?" asked Dawn.

"I have," said Kimber. "There's a girl named Maple Tree in one of my Green Grass books!"

"If Maple married Mr. Syrup she would be called Maple Syrup," laughed Shawn.

"I have one," said Janet. "If Holly married Mr. Bush, she would be called Holly Bush."

"I have another one," said Kimber. "If Lima married Mr. Bean she would be called Lima Bean." Everyone laughed thinking of Brooks and Lima Bean.

"You can't only use girls' names in this game. How about boys' names?" asked Dawn.

Warren responded, "Then we say, if Mr. and Mrs. Mountain had a boy and they named him Rocky, he would be Rocky Mountain."

"Just look at that stupid idiot," blasted Warren.

"Warren," Janet snapped at him. Warren rephrased his statement with a little bit of mockery.

"Just look at that impolite guy, driving on the shoulder trying to cut in ahead of everyone else. Well, he's not going to cut ahead of me." Warren honked his horn at the impolite driver. "What do you think Big Uid in the Sky would do to him?"

"He would pick up the impolite guy's car with his big hand," snickered Shawn, "and go vroom, vroom, vroom with the car on his other hand to get it revved up and then put the car down into a muddy field."

Warren chuckled. "I bet he would have a big towing bill to get his car out of that muddy field. I like this Big Uid in the Sky. What else does he do?"

"He likes to play demolition derby with black and white cars," Shawn said, laughing. "My dad said if you just say that Big Uid in the Sky will get someone that is irritating on the road, you don't get mad."

"I think that's a good idea. Don't you, Warren?" said Janet.

"Grandpa, I smell smoke back here," said Shawn.

"I smell it, too," said Janet.

"I do, too. I think the van is burning," said Warren. "I'm going to pull over and I want everyone to click off their seat belts as soon as the van comes to a stop. Shawn, you get Andrew out of his car seat and carry him as far away from the van as you can. Janet, you and Dawn get out and stay with Shawn. I'll make sure Kimber gets out." Warren brought the van to a stop and everyone went into action.

"Grandpa!" cried Kimber. "I can't get my seat belt undone!"

"It's okay. I'll be right there, Kimber." He slipped in beside her and pushed on the seat belt buckle release button but it would not come loose. He tried pulling the buckle away with all his strength but it would not budge.

"Hurry, Grandpa. It's getting hot and I'm scared," Kimber cried.

"I'll have you out in a minute, sweetheart," he said trying to keep his fear from his voice. He took out the Boy Scout knife he always carried in his pocket and began to cut away at the belt.

"Hurry, Grandpa! I don't want to burn up," Kimber was sobbing hysterically now. The sweat was running down Warren's face as he frantically sawed away at the belt. Finally it came lose and he backed out of the van dragging Kimber. He scooped her up into his arms just as smoke filled the inside of the van. Still holding Kimber, he ran from the van and leaned against a fence. He was breathing heavily from the exertion.

"Warren, are you all right?" Janet asked in alarm.

"I'm fine. I just have to catch my breath."

"Grandpa," said Kimber, recovering from her sobs, "you can let me go now."

Warren had not realized he was still clinging tightly onto her. "Oh, I'm sorry, sweetheart," he said through heavy breathing. "Are you okay?"

"I think so. You saved my life."

The group all clung to the fence in silence watching the burning van and thinking what could have happened. Several people had stopped, attempting to put out the fire with small fire extinguishers, but they were no match for a fire this large. A highway patrolman pulled up on his motorcycle. He moved the good Samaritans away from the burning van and walked over to Warren to make sure everyone was all right.

"I think we're fine—just very frightened."

"The fire department is on the way," the patrolman said. "Will you be able to find a ride home?"

"Yes," said Warren. "I'll work on that right now."

"Good," said the patrolman. "You did the smart thing and got your family out of the vehicle and as far away as possible."

"Thank you, officer," Warren said.

"No problem; you stay safe."

Warren pulled out his wallet and took out George's personal card. "Janet, do you have the cell phone?"

"No, it's still in your pocket."

"Oh, you're right, it is." He keyed in the car dealership's number with shaky fingers.

A very cheery voice answered. "Deal Dealership, can I help you?"

"I want to talk to George Hill," Warren said gruffly.

"I'm sorry, he's with a customer," said the cheery voice. "May I give you his voice mail?"

"No," Warren said sternly. "This is an emergency and I need to talk to him right now."

"May I get someone else to help you, sir?" The voice was not so cheery now.

"If you don't want to hear from my lawyer you will get him on the phone right this minute," snapped Warren. "Hello? Hello? Are you there? I think she hung up on me," said Warren.

"You were very gruff with her," said Janet. "It's not her fault the van caught on fire."

"You're right. I'll try to be nicer." He dialed the number again.

"Deal Dealership, how may I help you?" The voice sounded a little dejected this time.

"This is Warren Chapman and I really need to talk to George," he said, with a more pleasant voice. "The van he insisted I take for a test drive is on fire as we speak. My wife and I and four grandchildren are stranded on the freeway."

"Oh, I'm so sorry. I hope you're okay," she said alarmed. "Let me have your number and I will have him call you right back."

"Warren, you didn't apologize to her," said Janet.

"She hung up so fast she didn't give me a chance. But I was nicer to her."

A few minutes later the cell phone rang. Warren answered and said sharply, "Is this George?"

"Warren, how are you doing? Are you having a great time in the big comfortable SUV?" asked George in his best salesman voice.

"George, do you hear the sirens?" asked Warren as he pointed the cell phone towards the sound. "What you hear are three fire trucks just arriving to put out the burning pile of junk van you forced us to test drive. And furthermore, I barely got my granddaughter out in time because the seat belt buckle malfunctioned. I had to cut the belt with my pocket knife while smoke was coming inside the van. George, I'm just a little upset; so what are you going to do about it?" barked Warren.

George's salesman's voice disappeared and with great concern he asked. "Warren, I hope no one got hurt."

"We're fine, but we're stranded here on the freeway."

"I will personally come and pick you and your family up and take you home. Where are you?" asked George.

"We are on Highway 50, about two miles east of the Folsom turnoff."

"Warren," Janet said softly. "You need to calm down. I think you are scaring the children."

Kimber was crying. "It's all right, Kimber," said Janet. "It's only a big old van."

"But our mother's presents are in there," she managed to say through sobs. "And we got you a present, too, Grandma."

"Oh, how sweet," Janet said, as she dabbed at Kimber's tears with a hanky. "But when did you have time to buy me a gift? I was with you the whole time."

"Not when Andrew was throwing the tennis balls." Shawn announced, with a grin on his face.

Janet looked at the others and they were also grinning sheepishly. Andrew was grinning ear to ear and clapping his hands.

The joyful smile dropped from Janet's face into a long serious one. "Don't tell me you put him up to that mischief with the tennis balls," she asked.

"I guess we're guilty. But it worked," said Warren.

"Oh, I can't believe you did that. And to think I almost gave Andrew a spanking. I'm so sorry, Andrew. I didn't know they put you up to it." Andrew walked over and put his little arms around Janet and gave her a big hug.

"This is so exciting! Did you see how fast they put the fire out, Grandpa?" asked Shawn. "If I don't make it as a pro baseball player, I think I want to be a fireman." Shawn grinned with glee watching the firefighters in action. Then he started to laugh.

"What's so funny?" asked Kimber.

"I'm laughing because," and he looked at Dawn, "You don't have to make applesauce now; the fire already made it for you." Everyone broke into laughter—even Dawn had to laugh.

"We learned in church that if you sing, you will feel better," said Kimber. She started to sing a song she learned in church and the other children joined in with her. Warren and Janet were so impressed with their singing that they made the children sing until George got there.

When George showed up, he was driving an identical van to the one that was now a charred mess on the shoulder of the freeway. Warren grabbed George's arm tightly and grumbled in his ear, "Poor choice of vehicle, George. It's just like the van you gave us."

"I'm sorry; it was the only one available on short notice that would accommodate your big family," George said.

"You mean to tell me that out of all the vehicles on that lot this was the only one available?" snapped Warren.

"Well, I didn't remember what SUV I gave you," George confessed.

"I'm not getting into that van," cried Kimber, "It's just like the one I was almost burned up in. It will catch on fire and maybe this time I won't get out."

George was hit with the tragic reality of what might have happened and it showed on his face. He kneeled down so he could see face to face with Kimber and told her that it's very rare that an automobile catches on fire. "I promise you this van will not catch on fire."

Kimber looked at Warren for reassurance. "He's right, sweetheart. This was a very rare occasion and we'll be just fine on the way home."

"But what if my seat belt won't come undone?" she asked with teary eyes.

"I have never heard of a seat belt not coming undone before," said Warren. "But we will test the belt several times before we click you into it." She was still very reluctant but finally got into the van.

The ride home was quiet except for George trying to lighten the mood with lots of small talk and telling jokes.

"George," demanded Warren when they reached the Chapman driveway, "I want my car back and I want it delivered to my house tomorrow morning."

George could do nothing but say "Yes, sir. I'll have it here bright and early."

Chapter 20

Taking Your Money

"Hi, Mom," said Linda as she strolled into the kitchen.

"Did you get enough beauty sleep? It's almost lunch time," asked Janet, as she was icing a batch of sugar cookies.

"I had a late flight last night," Linda answered. "My high school French finally paid off! I got to do a flight to Paris. Who are you making the sugar cookies for?"

"The twins have been invited to a birthday party down the street, so I thought it would be nice if they took cookies," answered Janet.

"But Mom, won't they have birthday cake? I'm surprised you're not making apple cookies. Didn't you all go to Apple Hill yesterday? And where is that big ugly van? I didn't see it in the drive way."

"Oh, the most terrible thing happened. It caught on fire and burned up!" answered her mother.

"Good. At least Daddy can't buy it now."

114

"It burned up with all the stuff we bought at Apple Hill," she said, looking up from the cookies.

"That's not good; that's not good! Is everyone okay?"

"Yes, we're fine, but your father had a hard time getting Kimber out of the van. He had to cut the seat belt away from her and they got out just in time."

"That's really awful. Poor girl. I bet she was scared to death," said Linda.

"She was hysterical and your father was physically shaken, too. He was a hero. I used to always tease him about that pocketknife he's carried in his pocket ever since he was a Boy Scout. But I won't anymore."

"How's she doing?" asked Linda.

"She's been busy practicing for her recital."

"What recital?"

"Her ballet recital," Janet said.

"How can she be in a recital already?"

"I told you. I take her every day for a lesson. The ballet instructor says she is so good that if I continue her lessons every day she'll be ready for the beginner's recital."

"Mom! They're just draining you of your money," said Linda.

"No, she is really good and she loves it. She is probably out by the pool practicing right now while the other children are swimming. Remember when you were her age and you wore that cute little pink ballet costume—the one with the rhinestones on the front? You looked so adorable in it. Your father and I were so proud of you."

"I know, I know. Dad took a million pictures."

"I think you still have that costume in your closet. Do you think it would fit Kimber?"

"I have lots of my old ballet costumes stuffed in the back of my closet. I haven't looked at them in years."

"Maybe after lunch you could get them out and show them to Kimber. I think she would love to see them. But right now, help me bag up these cookies and then you can help me get lunch ready."

****

After lunch Linda asked Kimber, "Would you like to see some of my old ballet costumes?"

Kimber said, "I sure would!" She followed Linda into her bedroom. She sat on the bed while Linda rummaged through the back of her closet. "Can I help you?" Kimber asked.

"No, no, I think I've found them." Linda brought out a big box and set it on the floor. Kimber jumped off the bed and watched as Linda opened the box. Kimber jumped up and down with excitement when she saw all the ballet costumes.

"Oh!" gasped Kimber. "That pink one is just like the costumes we're wearing for the recital!"

"Would you like to try it on?" asked Linda.

"Oh, could I?"

Linda helped Kimber put on the little pink costume and zipped it up the back. Kimber turned around so Linda could look at her. "Oh, Kimber, it fits you perfectly!"

The family was still sitting at the patio table when Linda joined them. "Kimber is going to show us how she looks in her new dance costume," said Linda as she sat down with them. They all waited for Kimber and they were not disappointed. She came out walking the ballet strut that ballerinas use when they walk on the stage to pose before they start their dance.

"You look adorable!" exclaimed Janet.

"All you need to do now is put your hair up and you will look perfect," said Linda.

"Do you want to see her dance?" Janet looked at Linda. Before Linda could answer, Kimber ran and turned on the music and started her dance routine. When she was done, everyone cheered and clapped wildly.

"Wow! Kimber you really are good," said Linda. "There is only one thing. You need to relax your mouth and not scrunch it up."

Kimber ran over to Linda and threw her arms around her and gave her a great big hug "Thank you so much for letting me use this beautiful ballet costume, Linda. I love you."

"I will need to send the costume to the cleaners," said Janet. "The tutu part looks a little limp."

Kimber turned to Janet and also gave her a big hug. "Grandma, thank you so much for taking me to ballet lessons. I love you so much."

Janet looked at her newly-adopted granddaughter and smiled. "I love you too, Kimber." Janet thought to herself, *"This is a perfect moment."*

Chapter 21

Grandma's Roses

"Tomorrow is Grandma's birthday," said Warren to Dawn and Kimber as they set the table on the back patio for dinner. "I've given her a rose bush every year for the last fifteen years for her birthday. So I thought we could go to the garden shop and pick out a rose bush for this year."

"That would be great," said Kimber. "The present we got her at Apple Hill burned up in that terrible old van."

"Grandpa, you said fifteen years but I only count thirteen rose bushes," said Dawn. "Where are the other two?"

"There were a couple of rose bushes that didn't survive, so I replaced them with a new one on her next birthday," answered Warren.

"Grandpa," said Kimber. "What other color rose can we get? She has every color already and two of some colors and there are three white ones."

"That's true, but each white rose bush is different and has it's own name. Come look at them." Warren walked over to a bush that had a beautiful pure white rose. Kimber followed him and stopped in front of it. "This is a long-stem variety with only one rose on the stem. Smell it."

"It smells really good," said Kimber.

"It's called Full Sail," said Warren, as he pointed to a little metal plaque that stuck out of the ground. "I made a plaque for each bush with the name and the year we planted it."

The little group walked over to the next white rose bush. "This one has lots of little roses on the same stem," said Dawn.

"And it doesn't smell as good. I like the other one better," said Kimber.

"Where are you going to plant a new rose bush? There isn't any more room out here," said Dawn.

"Don't you worry! Your Grandmother always finds a place for a new rose bush," he answered.

"What's going on out here," said Janet as she set a big dish of enchiladas on the table. "And what happened to my helpers?"

"Grandpa was just showing us your roses," said Dawn.

"My roses are so beautiful. I just love them. They are God's gift to us."

＊＊＊＊＊＊＊＊＊＊＊＊

As Warren, Dawn, and Kimber walked into the garden shop, a tall man with gray hair and dirt under his fingernails greeted Warren warmly. "I knew you'd be here, so I've set aside some new rose bushes. I see you brought your list."

"Yep, I have to have the list. I can't remember all the names of the roses I bought and I don't want to buy a duplicate."

"And who are these pretty young ladies with you?" asked Mr. Schultz.

"They are my granddaughters. Girls, this is Mr. Schultz. He has helped me pick out all the rose bushes the last fifteen years. In fact, the rose tradition was all his idea."

"I wish I could take the credit for the idea," said Mr. Schultz. "But it was actually Mrs. Chapman who told me to tell you to buy a rose bush for her birthday. She said that you weren't so good at getting her birthday presents."

"I didn't know that," said Warren. "It was her idea?"

"After all these years, I thought you knew," Mr. Schultz said, a little embarrassed.

"No, I didn't know. But it doesn't matter because it makes her happy."

"Grandpa, look at this rose. It's called 'Barbara Streisand,'" said Dawn. "I love the purple color and it smells so good."

"Let me check the list. Here it is on the list. I bought that one two years ago."

"Grandpa, look at this one. It says 'Kiss Me.'" Kimber bent down and kissed the delicate pink rose blossom. "It smells really good, too."

"I don't think that one is on the list, but let me look. Nope! That's a new one. Maybe we should buy it."

"What a minute!" Dawn said with excitement. "I've found the perfect rose! Come look at this one."

"It's pink like the one I picked out, but it's so small," said Kimber. "I like mine better."

Dawn was beaming now and replied, "But this one is called 'Grandma's Blessing.'"

"Kimber, I think Dawn is right. 'Grandma's Blessing' is perfect. We will take four of them," said Warren.

"Four? Why so many?" questioned Mr. Schultz.

"I want one for each of our four grandchildren."

Chapter 22

Fountain Monster

"There's the restaurant right there on the left. It's the building that looks like the Roman coliseum," said Janet.

Warren switched to the left lane and turn into the parking lot. "It looks expensive to me."

"My buddy, Betty, told me about it, so you know it's not expensive," she said. "It's a family restaurant."

As the little birthday celebration group entered the large waiting area of the restaurant they were amazed at the sight before them.

"Wow, this place is awesome," said Shawn. "It's like being in another world."

On the wall to the right was a long colonnade with large round columns that almost reached to the ceiling. The ceiling was painted to look like a blue sky with white fluffy clouds. There were benches in and around the colonnade for families to sit while waiting to be seated for dinner and every bench was full of people.

"This place is packed. We'll probably have to wait forever to eat," complained Warren.

"I made a reservation, so don't worry," answered Janet. She walked up to a reception counter that looked like the back of a Roman chariot driven by a gladiator. The gladiator had reins in his left hand and his right hand had a whip raised over his head. Another gladiator stood beside him with a shield in one hand and a sword in the other. The chariot was pulled by two full-sized horse statues leaping in action.

"We only have about a ten-minute wait," said Janet.

"Grandma, can we go look at the big water fountain?" asked Kimber.

"Sure, I'd like to get a better look at it myself. Warren, would you pick Andrew up and keep a tight grip on him, please?"

On the wall across from the colonnade was a huge water fountain. In the center of the fountain was a statue of a man standing in a large seashell. Just below him, standing on a rock formation were two statues of men each holding onto a horse. Water was flowing over the rock formation in several places.

"This fountain looks like the picture on the wall in the bedroom we sleep in," said Kimber.

"It is the same. It's the Trevi Fountain in Rome," answered Dawn.

"You're right! April took that picture when she was in Rome," said Janet. "Look! There's a plaque telling about the fountain. Dawn would you read what it says?"

"Trevi Fountain was built by Pope Clement XII. Work began in 1732, and the fountain was completed in 1762. The central figure is Neptune sculpted by Pietro Bracci.

"What does the other plaque say?" asked Kimber.

Dawn continued. "This is an imitation of the Trevi Fountain in Rome. The tradition is if you throw a coin over your left shoulder into the fountain, you will return to eat here again."

"That's a clever way to get you to come back," remarked Warren.

"I guess a lot of people must come back because there are tons of coins," said Shawn. "I bet if someone was to get in and pick up all those coins it would pay for their dinner!"

A young girl with long brown hair accented with a wreath of white daisies approached Janet and said, "Mrs. Chapman, your table for six is ready." She was dressed in a long white tunic with a gold braided rope around her waist.

Out of the corner of her eye Dawn was watching her brother. He was staring at the young girl with his mouth partly open. As they walked to their table Dawn teased him by whispering in his ear. "She's real cute."

Shawn bristled and grumbled, "I didn't notice."

When everyone got settled into a large booth, a young man came over and smiled at them. He was also dressed in a tunic with a leather strap tied around his waist and leather sandals with laces crisscrossed all the way up to just below his knees.

"My name is Antonio and I'm your server tonight. We have two menus. This one is a family-style menu," he said as he handed it to Warren. "You can order large plates of several items, such as spaghetti, ravioli, lasagna, pizza, and so on. A salad, garlic bread, and desert are included. Also, if the lady," he handed a menu to Janet, "would like to order something like eggplant parmesan, she can order it as a side order from our other menu. It is the full dinner menu, which includes the soup and salad bar, a pasta bar, and specialty deserts. Are there any questions?"

"I don't have any questions. Everything sounds great to me," said Shawn.

"What's for dessert?" asked Kimber.

"With the family dinner, it's Spumoni ice cream."

"What kind of ice cream is that?" asked Kimber.

Dawn answered before the waiter could. "It's ice cream with candied fruits and nuts in it."

"Are you showing off for the waiter?" Shawn whispered in his sister's ear. Dawn blushed and glared at him.

"I can take your drink orders now and you can decide what you want to order for dinner," said Antonio.

"Are the drinks included in the family dinner?" asked Warren.

"No, those are extra."

"We'll all have water," replied Warren.

"Warren, it's my birthday and I'd like something to drink besides water," complained Janet.

"Me, too," said Kimber. "I want a Shirley Temple."

Warren sighed and said, "Okay, you all can order something, but I'm going to drink water."

After the drinks were ordered, Kimber asked, "Grandma, where are you going to plant your birthday roses?"

"I know the perfect place. If Warren and Shawn will dig out the raggedy old juniper plants between the sidewalk and front porch before they go to the baseball game tomorrow, then we ladies can plant the roses while they're gone. I want my 'Grandma's Blessing' roses there because that is the first place I saw you four children." She smiled at them. "This has been such a wonderful birthday."

"Grandpa, after dinner can we throw a coin in the fountain?" asked Kimber.

"Only if the food is good, because I don't want to come back if it's not!" he answered.

The waiter came back with the drinks and asked if they were ready to order dinner.

"I think if we order three items from the Family Menu it will be enough to feed all of us," said Janet.

"Maybe all but Shawn," chuckled Warren. "Janet, it's your birthday, so you order something you want."

"Okay, but I'll see what the children order first, then I will order something."

The children put in their orders and Shawn said, "Grandma, you're not going to order that eggplant parmesan, are you?"

"No, I'm going to order a BBQ chicken pizza."

****

After everyone had finished eating, Warren teased Shawn, "Did you get enough to eat? There's more lasagna left."

"I couldn't eat another bite," answered Shawn.

"I can't believe it! I do think we finally filled him up," Janet replied smiling.

"I bet he'll have room for birthday cake later," piped Kimber.

"Kimber! That was supposed to be a surprise," said Dawn.

Janet smiled at the girls. "Andrew, you're squirming around. Do you need to go to the rest room?"

Andrew nodded 'yes.'

"I'll take him," said Shawn.

The restrooms were next to the Trivi Fountain. "Okay, Andrew, you go first and then you can wait for me."

When Andrew was finished, Shawn told him again to wait for him and then he'd help him wash his hands.

"Andrew, are you still there?" Shawn asked. There was no response. "Andrew! Answer me! You had better still be there," said Shawn.

But there was no answer because Andrew had slipped out the restroom door and was in the Trivi Fountain pool collecting coins and putting them in his pockets.

"Andrew!" yelled Shawn. "What are you doing?"

Andrew ignored his brother and kept stuffing coins in his pockets. It was getting difficult for him to wade around because his pockets were getting heavy from all the coins, but he trudged on. The young hostess had heard Shawn's yell and saw Andrew in the fountain. She kicked off her shoes and stepped into the fountain and made her way towards Andrew. She put her hand on his shoulder and said something to him. He pulled away from her but lost his balance and down he went. She grabbed Andrew by the back of his shirt and pulled him up. He came up but his shorts didn't because they were so heavy with coins in the pockets. There he stood in his little white briefs.

Shawn wasn't yelling anymore. He was mortified and embarrassed that something like this had happened in front of the cute young hostess. Andrew reached down, pulled up his shorts, and scuffled towards Shawn. The hostess helped him keep his balance by holding on to the back of his shirt.

Warren had paid the bill and the rest of the family arrived at the fountain just in time to see Andrew escorted out of the pool. Shawn was humiliated, but he did manage to apologize and thank the hostess. He turned to Warren and said, "I'm so sorry I didn't watch him closer."

It was hard for Warren to keep a straight face looking at Andrew dripping wet holding up his sagging shorts. Andrew let go of his shorts with one of his hands, reached into his pocket and brought out a fist full of coins. He held them out to Warren.

"I think he wants to pay for Grandma's birthday dinner," said Shawn.

"Oh, Andrew," said Janet. "How can you be so naughty and so lovable at the same time?"

As they walked out of the restaurant Warren said, "I'm sure glad we didn't throw a coin in the fountain because I don't think they want us to come back."

Chapter 23

Close Call

Later that night after the children had gone to bed a police car pulled up in front of the Chapman house. Shawn heard the car and looked out the window. He ran to the girl's room. "Dawn! Wake up! We need to leave," he said as he shook her out of a sound sleep.

"Shawn, what's wrong? Why do we need to leave?"

"There's a police car out front. I'll get Andrew. You wake up Kimber and meet me in the back yard."

"Wake up, Kimber! We need to go," said Dawn as she pulled her little sister out of bed.

"Where are we going? It's still dark. It's not time to get up."

"Just be quiet and come with me." They crept down the hall to a bathroom that opened onto the backyard patio. Shawn was by the side gate watching for her.

"We can hide in the bushes on the school yard," he said.

Dawn tried to open the gate. "The gate's locked; so now what do we do?"

"Don't worry. I know where Grandpa hides the key," said Shawn.

Dawn looked at him with a disbelieving face.

"Don't look at me that way. I have a brain you know. I found out where the key was just in case we had a situation like this—in case we needed an escape plan. It's under the wooden pelican."

"Dawn, please don't just stand there! Get the key. I have my arms full with Andrew."

Dawn opened the gate and they all headed for the bushes. Shawn laid the sleeping Andrew gently on the ground so he was hidden in the bushes. Kimber sat next to him, shivering.

"I'm scared," she sobbed.

"Shawn, do you think the Chapmans called the police?" ask Dawn.

"No, Grandpa wouldn't do that. I think it was the nosey lady in the house across the street. I always see her peeking through the window curtains. I bet she is peeking through them right now. You stay here with Andrew and Kimber. I'm going to go watch to see when the police leave."

"The police," sobbed Kimber. "I don't want to go to jail."

"I won't let anyone take you to jail." Shawn gave his sister a small hug.

"Shawn, do you think you should call Aunt Jackie?" asked Dawn.

"No, not yet," he replied as he disappeared into the darkness.

＊＊＊＊＊＊＊＊＊＊＊＊

Meanwhile, Warren answered the door to find a policeman standing there.

"Are you Mr. Chapman?" asked the policeman.

"Yes, I am. Is something wrong officer?"

"I got a report that a mother abandoned her kids at this address. Is that true, Mr. Chapman?"

"There are children here, but the mother is a co-worker of my daughter, April, and we are caring for the children until their mother returns from vacation."

"So there isn't any problem?' ask the policeman.

"No, sir, everything is just fine."

"Sorry I bothered you so late," replied the policeman.

"Warren, who was that at the door?" asked Janet.

"It was the police asking about the children, but I sent him away."

"I'm so glad the children are in bed because I wouldn't want them to be frightened," replied Janet. "I think I'll go check on them."

****

Shawn was running to hide in the next bush when a bright light shined past him. He threw himself underneath the bush as if he was sliding into home base and lay very quiet, listening for footsteps of the police officer. He felt his heart pounding and he was gripped with fear. He thought to himself, *"I've failed and ruined everything. The police will take us away and Mother will get in trouble and Dawn will never let me forget that it was my fault."* But he didn't hear footsteps; he heard voices. He cautiously peaked between branches of the bush and saw the police officer talking to the nosey lady across the street. He also saw that the bright light was the headlight of the police car and luckily not shining where he was hiding, so he was safe. He watched as the officer got in his car and drove away.

****

"Warren, the children are gone!" Janet blurted.

"They are? Maybe they're in the backyard watching shooting stars."

They hurried to the backyard and called out the children names.

Warren went over to the gate and discovered it was unlocked. "Janet, I think they went out the gate."

Janet ran over to him in a panic, "Why would they do that?"

"It's okay, Janet; there they are." He pointed to the children making their way back toward the gate. Shawn was holding Andrew. Lucky he had slept through the entire ordeal.

Kimber saw Janet and ran into her arms and said, "I was so scared. I didn't want to go to jail."

Janet held Kimber close to her. "I would never ever let anyone take you to jail, sweetheart."

Chapter 24

I Don't Want to Go

Dawn and Shawn where sitting on the edge of the pool when she asked her brother, "Have you talked to Mom lately?"

"A couple days ago. We've been so busy and I'm so tired at night, I can't stay awake long enough to call her," he admitted.

"You had better call tonight; she's probably wondering about us. Our two weeks will be up tomorrow," Dawn reminded, with a frown on her face.

"I know," he replied. "This has been the best vacation ever. Do you think she'll let us come back and visit the Chapmans?"

"I don't know; it's against the rules of The Family Game. But we can ask her," Dawn said with hopefulness in her voice.

Kimber swam up to her siblings. "What are you talking about? You look sad."

"It's time to go home," answered Dawn.

"I don't want to go home," Kimber announced.

"I know; we don't want to leave either, but we'll probably go home Friday night," said Shawn.

"NO! We can't go home Friday night," Kimber wailed.

"Our two weeks are over on Friday. We have to go," said Shawn.

"No!" cried Kimber louder. "*We can't! We just can't!*" She was sobbing now.

"I'm sorry, Kimber, but we have no choice," Dawn said.

"My recital is Saturday night and I can't miss my recital," Kimber managed to say between sobs.

"Oh, that's right, it is. Shawn you will just have to talk Mother into letting us stay one more night."

"I'll try my best," said Shawn".

"Maybe I should talk to her," Dawn demanded.

"No!" said Shawn. "Mom said I was in charge of the phone calls. I will call her."

"You'd better do a good job of talking her into letting us stay until Saturday night," she retorted.

★★★★★★★★★★★★

"Hi, Mom," said Shawn when his mother answered the phone.

"Why haven't you called me?" she snapped at him. "I've been worried."

"I'm sorry, Mom, we've just been so busy and I couldn't stay awake long enough to call."

What she wanted to say to her son was, "*Yeah, too busy having so much fun with the Chapmans instead of me.*" But she held her tongue and said, "I really miss you children and I can't wait to see you. I'll be in front of the Chapmans' house tomorrow night at 2 a.m."

"Mom, can we stay one more night and meet you Saturday night?"

"No!" she said, "I can't wait one more day. I want you home with me."

"But Mom, Kimber has a ballet recital Saturday night. Please don't make her miss it, Mom. It will break her heart," he pleaded.

Laura's mood softened. She was pleased with her son's concern about his little sister. "A ballet recital?" she asked. "How can she be in a ballet recital?"

"Grandma takes her to lessons every day."

"Shawn, did you forget the rule about not letting the adopted grandparents spend a lot of money on all of you?"

"I know, but this time it's different."

Laura had sensed it was different this time and it frightened her. She felt she was losing her children to strangers. But she didn't want to break Kimber's heart. "Where is the recital and what time?" she asked her son.

He told her.

"I want you to be in front of the house Saturday night at 2 a.m. And don't forget you are not to bring home any of the things they've bought for you. It's the rules of the game," she reminded him.

"Okay, Mom, thanks. We'll see you at 2 a.m."

Laura thought, *"Maybe it's a good thing I have one more day without the children. I can give the apartment a good cleaning."*

Their home was a nice apartment: two bedrooms, one bath, a front room, dining area, and a kitchen. The apartment didn't really have a front door. It had a covered carport next to a small courtyard. Everyone always entered the apartment at the kitchen door from the courtyard, which was more like a back door. There was a sliding glass door off the front room that opened onto a small cement patio. Where the patio ended was a large grassy area. All the apartments' front-room doors opened onto the grassy area. It was a nice place for the children to play. The two bedrooms were larger than in most standard apartments. Laura had fit twin beds in one of the bedrooms where Shawn and Andrew slept. She put a queen bed in her room and Kimber slept with her. Dawn slept on the fold-down sofa in the front room. Laura had found used furniture that was still in good condition at a thrift store. She had taken interior design classes before she married Christian, so the way she decorated the apartment was something the children could be proud of.

Chapter 25

The Pick Up

Laura slipped into the crowded small auditorium. All the seats were taken so she stood by the door. She could barely see the Chapmans and her children sitting up closer to the front. She was nervous because she didn't want them to see her. Fortunately, the beginner classes danced first and she was able to leave after Kimber danced without being seen. She marveled at the grace and beauty her little girl showed while she danced. She was really very good and it seemed to come so naturally to her. Laura knew somehow she had to find a way for Kimber to continue dance lessons.

****

Later that night, Laura parked a little way from the Chapman house watching for the children to come out. She was so anxious to see her children that she arrived fifteen minutes early just in case they were out before 2 a.m. She didn't want them to be waiting so late at night. The wait seemed like forever, but right on time she saw her children come into view. She got out of the car and ran toward them. Andrew spotted his mother and ran into her arms. Kimber was next and then Dawn and Shawn all created a family group hug.

"We'd better get into the car before someone sees us," said Laura. As Laura drove away she sensed that the children were too quiet. "I'm really glad to see you," said Laura to her children. "I've missed you so much. I don't think I can go through this Family Game again."

"We don't want to do The Family Game anymore either," said Dawn.

"You don't? Didn't you enjoy being with the Chapmans?" She was secretly hoping maybe their stay wasn't all fun.

"Oh, we loved being with them! And...we want to go back and visit them again," said Shawn with more emotion than Laura had expected from him.

Laura didn't know what to say, but she knew she had to remind them of the rules of The Family Game. Very gently she said, "You know it's against the rules to revisit the grandparents. Remember, you children made the rules. You've never wanted to revisit the other grandparents."

"We know, Mom, but if we're not going to play the game anymore, can't we change the rules?" asked Shawn.

"Mommy," said Kimber. "Mrs. Chapman took me to ballet lessons every day so I could be in a dance recital. I know she loves me."

"Mr. Chapman took me to baseball games and helped me with my batting," Shawn said. "He will miss me as much as I'll miss him."

"And I'm learning to cook," said Dawn. "Mrs. Chapman makes it fun."

"We want to go back," pleaded Kimber. "You can go with us, Mommy. They will love you just like they love us."

Laura's eyes filled with tears. She was feeling that jealousy again because she had not had to share her children's love since their father's death. "I'm not sure it's such a good idea to go back," said Laura. "Don't you remember? We discussed going back when we made the rules of the game."

Out of the darkness came a defiant little voice that had never been heard before, "I want my grandpa!"

"Andrew! Was that you?" Laura asked with surprise as all the children looked at Andrew.

He answered louder this time, "I want my grandpa!"

The rest of the children were all cheering and clapping their hands. "Well, Mommy, Andrew said something very important, just like the doctor said he would," Kimber declared.

Chapter 26

He Thinks We're Criminals

"Warren, get up! The children are gone!" cried Janet.

"What do you mean they're gone? What time is it?" asked Warren.

"It's 4:30 a.m.," she blurted. "They're gone. I can't find them anywhere."

"Did you look in the backyard? Maybe they are watching for shooting stars," he said still half asleep. Janet seized onto any glimmer of hope and ran out of the bedroom and down the hall headed for the backyard. Warren pulled himself out of bed and followed after her.

"They're not here and the gate's locked," she said. She slumped down onto a lawn chair.

He sat beside her on another chair. "You knew this was going to happen. They had to leave sometime," he said trying to comfort her.

"I know, but I didn't think it would be so soon."

"It's been two weeks and they have to go back to school," he said.

They sat there awhile, both wrapped up in their own thoughts. Janet broke the silence. "I thought at least their mother would come to the door to get them. We could have told her how wonderful her children are and asked her if they could come stay with us once in a while."

"I know, Janet. I just don't understand their mother. She is a strange one." Warren got up and took Janet's hand and said, "Come on, let's go back to bed." He held her in his arms but neither of them fell asleep.

∗∗∗∗∗∗∗∗∗∗∗∗

Janet didn't get up to make breakfast as she usually did. She didn't even get out of bed. She had not been this devastated for a very long time—not since before she met Warren. He had brought her happiness and their children had been the delight of her life. She had always wanted to be a mother and live out her days spoiling her grandchildren. The last two weeks she had been in her element and she thrived on it.

Warren waited until he thought Janet might be awake before he came into their bedroom. "Janet, the children left us notes." Each child had written a note addressed to Grandma and Grandpa. Dawn had written one for Andrew.

> Grandma, I will miss the good food you cook. Grandpa, I will miss going to the baseball games and watching them on TV with you. I'm leaving the season tickets because I won't have anyone to take me. Love, Shawn.

> Dear Grandma, I'll miss the cooking lessons and all the great discussions we had on subjects we both liked. Grandpa, you try to be gruff, but I know you're really a sweetheart. Hugs, Dawn.

Grandma, thank you for the ballet lessons. They were my dream come true. Grandpa, thank you for saving my life. I love you both so much! Kimber.

Grandma, I like your pancakes. Grandpa, I'll miss climbing on your lap and falling asleep. A.

It was even more hurtful to Janet when she discovered the children had left behind all the clothes, toys, and everything else the Chapmans had bought them. She blamed their mother. *"How could a mother just dump her children off for two weeks and then take them back without a word? How could she be so cruel to us? Letting us fall in love with her children and snatching them back. Who is she? Where are they? Why did she do this?"* She repeated it over and over in her mind.

Janet called the phone number the children gave her but it was disconnected.

Warren went to where his daughter, April, worked to find the children's mother. He learned her name was Laura and she had transferred to another agency. She requested that her new location not be revealed.

When they finally got hold of April in Africa, she told them the only thing she knew about Laura was her last name was Blaine, she had four children and their father had been killed in the war. April said, "Laura didn't talk much about her personal life, but she did ask tons of questions about you, Mom and Dad. She wanted to know what kind of parents I had, where they lived, if they worked, and if they went to church. Every day she would ask me more questions. When I asked her, 'Why all the questions?' she said, 'Oh it's nice to hear about loving parents and a stable family.'

"She even asked me if maybe my parents would babysit her children. I said I guess so. Laura was a very private person and I'm not sure if she had made friends with anyone else." April said she wouldn't know much more until she went back to work and talked to some of her co-workers.

Janet remembered that Dawn said they passed Heather Glenn Estates when their mother drove them to school. Warren and Janet drove to a school that was near Heather Glenn. They parked on a side street where they could watch the parents dropping off their children. After several days, the school security officer approached the car and asked what they were doing.

"We're looking for our grandchildren," answered Janet.

"Tell me their names and I will see if they are registered at the school," said the officer.

Warren told the officer the names and ages of the three older children.

The office said, "Stay here and I will check on the names. May I see your driver's license and car registration?"

When the officer walked away, Warren spoke first. "Maybe this will work out well. If we find out they're not here, we can go check another school."

Janet and Warren waited and reminisced on the some of the fun things they had done with the children.

"Mr. Chapman," the officer said, "The children's names you gave me are not registered at this school. I have run your license plate and driver's license and they seem to be clear, so I won't arrest you today. But if you and your wife come back again, I will arrest you for loitering in a school zone. Also, I have faxed your information and description to other schools in the Sacramento area. So I suggest you get out of here right now."

"Oh, good grief, Janet, he thinks we're criminals!" exclaimed Warren.

"Well, I guess you can't blame him," said Janet. "Don't you remember we built a house next to the school and put a gate in our fence so the children wouldn't have to go out onto the street?"

"I did that so they wouldn't get hit by a car while walking to school," he corrected her.

Warren and Janet had reached a dead end. They didn't know what to do next to find the children.

****

Warren was back in his easy chair watching baseball just like before he knew the children. They had stolen his heart and he missed them a lot more than he let on. He couldn't bring himself to go to the baseball games without Shawn. He missed little Andrew curling up on his lap and clinging onto him when he was supposed to go to bed. He missed bubbly little Kimber with that wonderfully witty personality. He missed seeing Janet teaching Dawn how to cook. They were happy as clams in the kitchen together. They delighted in trying new recipes. What joy it gave him watching the little family sit at the dinner table having marvelous conversations! He missed watching them swim in the pool. How could four little children, in two short weeks, cause such sadness in his world when they were gone? Warren had become grumpier than ever before.

Janet wasn't doing much better. She missed Shawn because he never failed to compliment her on what a good meal she cooked, although he never acknowledged his sister even though she was half of the cooking team. Oh, how she missed Dawn. What great times they had in the kitchen, cooking and jabbering, as Warren would call it. They never lacked for finding something to talk about. As hard as she tried, her own daughters never found cooking interesting or fun. She would tell them, "How are you ever going to catch a husband if you don't learn to cook?" They would always answer back, "We'll find a man who likes to cook, so we don't have to!"

What a delight it was to watch Kimber in her dance lessons. Kimber loved dancing and after each lesson she always hugged Janet and told her she loved her.

And she missed Andrew—despite all his mischievousness. She had watched as his sad eyes turned into smiling eyes. He had put on some weight in the two weeks she cared for him and he didn't look so unhealthy. And he had given up grape bubble gum for her. She wanted them back.

Chapter 27

Superburgers

Warren was watching a baseball game on TV, when he remembered Shawn telling him that the hamburgers at the baseball game were not as good as the Superburgers his mother brought home from work on Saturday. "*Was that the actual name of the hamburger or was it what Shawn called them because they were so good?*" Warren thought. "*Have I ever heard of a Superburger?*" He said "Superburger, Superburger" out loud trying to remember if he had ever heard of a Superburger and where they were sold.

"Superburger!" blared from the TV. "Come try a Superburger at Hardy Burger. Your life will never be the same. Superburger! The best hamburgers in the world." Warren stared at the TV in amazement. He jumped up out of his chair and looked in the phone book for the nearest Hardy Burger. There was one about two miles from his house. He grabbed the car keys and yelled at Janet. "I'll be back in a while."

144

And with that, he was out the door before she could ask where he was going.

Warren walked into the Hardy Burger and sat in a booth. A pleasant-looking lady came over and asked, "What will you have, Mister? But you better be fast."

"Does a Laura Blaine work here?"

"She does but she's not here tonight."

"Is she sick?" Warren asked with concern.

"No, she is at our other location on Fair Oaks."

"Thanks," he got up to leave.

"I don't think you can get there in time. They close in fifteen minutes," the pleasant looking lady said.

Warren looked at his watch. He hadn't realized it was so late. "Will she be here tomorrow night?"

"I don't know. I don't know her schedule. Sorry."

He thought to himself on the way home, *"It's probably better I didn't see her tonight because I haven't even thought what I would say to her."*

It took a long time for him to fall asleep that night. He had found the children's mother. Now what was he going to say to her?

****

The next day during breakfast he had a brilliant idea. "That's brilliant," he said under his breath.

"What did you say, dear?" his wife asked.

"Oh, nothing" he said. He gobbled down his breakfast and got up from the table.

"Warren, what is the matter with you? You've been acting so strangely and you seem to be preoccupied with something."

"I'm fine," Warren said, "I'll tell you about it later."

"If I wasn't in a hurry to get ready for my quilters guild, I'd make you tell me now, not later. We're having a quilt show and luncheon today. I won't be home until after two. There is plenty of lunch meat in the refrigerator for a sandwich." He glanced at the refrigerator, not because of lunch meat but to see if the Archer's invitation was still there and it was. "Warren, would you be a dear and clean up?"

Warren was glad she would be gone because he didn't want the third degree on where he was going. She had already given him the third degree about last night.

He picked up the phone and dialed Mrs. Archer's number. "Hello," answered Brooks, "this is the Archer residence."

"Hi, Brooks, this is Warren Chapman. Do you know if the pictures Mrs. Archer had taken at the dinner party are done?"

"You mean the portraits?" he corrected. "I don't know. I will ask Mrs. Archer. Please hold." Warren waited for what seemed like an eternity.

"Warren, I'm leaving now," called out Janet. "I'll see you later."

"Okay," he yelled back. "Have a good time."

"Mr. Chapman, are you still there?" came Brooks' dry voice from the phone.

"Yes, I'm here."

"Mrs. Archer says she has not heard from the photographer and doesn't know if the portraits are ready. Is that all, Mr. Chapman?"

"No," said Warren, with urgency, "I want the name and address of the photographer, please."

"Please hold. I'll have to find it," Brooks said with annoyance in his voice. Warren waited what seemed like another eternity before Brooks came back on the phone and gave him the name and address. Brooks hung up before Warren had a chance to say thank you.

Warren grabbed his set of car keys and headed for the garage. But when he got there the car was gone. "Where's the car?" he said out loud. Then it dawned on him—Janet took the car. "What am I going to do?" he said out loud again.

He walked back into the kitchen and stared out the window at the neighbor's garage wall, thinking what his next move would be. Then it hit him.

His neighbor, Cecil, answered the door. "Cecil, may I borrow your car for the day?" asked Warren. "I have an emergency."

"You want to use it right now?" Cecil asked.

"Yes, right now. I hope you don't need to use it today."

"No, I don't think so," replied Cecil.

"Great! Where are the keys?" Warren asked, as he pushed his way past Cecil and into the house.

"Warren, what's the emergency? Can I help?"

"No, I can handle it myself. I'll tell you later. I just need the keys."

Cecil gave him the keys and opened the garage door. "Warren, you be careful with my car; you seem agitated."

"I'm fine. I'm not agitated, I'm just..." and he drove away.

✳✳✳✳✳✳✳✳✳✳✳

Warren pulled into the strip mall and parked in front of the photograph shop. He asked the man standing behind the counter if the photos taken at Mrs. Archer's house were ready.

The man said, "Mrs. Archer, she is a very good customer. Let me check. What's the name of the family?"

"Chapman." Warren said impatiently.

"Oh, yes, here they are. Would you like to look at them?"

Warren grabbed the envelope and pulled out a dozen pictures. "Why are they all so small?" asked Warren."

"They're only proofs, sir. You pick out the picture you like the best from the proofs and then we will print the portrait."

Warren scanned the proofs and pointed at one he thought looked the best. "I'll take that one."

"What size would you like?" the man asked.

Warren looked around the studio and pointed at a family portrait he thought was the right size.

"That is 16 by 20 and will cost $48."

"$48?" said Warren with amazement.

"You can order the 11 by 14 portrait for $30, if you like."

"No, I want the big one. When can you have it ready?"

The man looked at the calendar and said, "Next Tuesday."

"No, that won't do. I need it today."

"That's impossible," said the man.

Warren took a hundred-dollar bill from his wallet and set it on the counter. "Will this get the job done in an hour?"

The man eyed the money and said, "Let me see what I can do." He disappeared into the back and came out a few minutes later, took the hundred-dollar bill, and said, "Sir, we can have it ready in two hours. Do you want a glossy or matte finish?"

"I don't know; whatever you think is best," said Warren. "And I'll need it framed."

"Oh, we don't do frames," the man said.

Warren's ease turned to worry. "So where can I get it framed?"

"There's a frame shop about five miles from here on the corner of Howe and Arden."

****

Warren entered the frame shop and saw a young girl with beautiful red hair. "*I like her already,*" he said to himself. "I need to frame a picture," he announced to her.

"Do you have the picture with you?" she asked.

"No, it's not ready yet, but it will be ready in two hours."

"What size frame do you want?"

"The picture is 16 by 20," he answered.

"There are some 16 by 20 frames on aisle 14," she told him.

He headed for aisle 14 and there were lots of frames that size. He had no idea what to choose. He picked up and looked at several frames, but he couldn't make up his mind. He went back to the same young lady for help. She was waiting on a customer and so he waited until she was done. "I'm sorry, but I'm not good at this type of thing. Could you help me?"

They both headed for aisle 14. "What type of picture are you framing?" she asked.

"It's a portrait of my grandchildren."

"Is it a formal or casual picture?" she asked.

"They look like they are going to a wedding."

"I'll say it's formal. Do you want a dark wood, light wood, or a metal frame?"

"I don't know," he said shaking his head.

"Let's take one of each and put them on the counter and you can study them for a while." She picked out three of the most formal looking frames and he carried them to the counter. There was another couple waiting to be helped when they arrived at the counter. They had a picture of their dog, a German shepherd. The young redhead girl helped them pick out a mat and frame. All the while Warren was watching. He heard the young lady say, "That will be eighty dollars for materials and framing." Warren caught his breath. They had just a little picture and he wondered what it would cost to frame his.

After the couple left, he asked her about the mat. She pointed out two pictures on the wall: one with a mat and one without a mat. "I think the picture with the mat looks the best," he said.

"I do, too," she agreed.

"I want my picture to have a mat," Warren decided.

"In that case, we will have to get a bigger frame to accommodate the mat. One that is 18 by 22 and they are on aisle 16." As he trudged to aisle 16, he thought, *"Why don't they put 16-inch frames on isle 16 and 18-inch frames on aisle 18. It would be much easier."* He picked out three frames he thought looked like the other ones. The little redhead was waiting on another customer. He wasn't quite sure what their picture was. The picture they had had red, orange, purple, and blue swirls on it with a big black circle in the middle.

After showing Warren all the different types of matting she told him to pick the texture he liked the best and she would help pick out the color when she saw the picture. There were now two more customers waiting in line for help. Warren looked at the mats but wasn't sure which one he liked. He waited and waited but the line just kept getting longer, so he decided to go get some lunch.

He didn't see the little redhead girl when he returned to the frame shop. Warren put the picture on the counter and a young man asked if the three frames were his. Warren nodded 'yes.' The young man placed the portrait inside each frame and they studied each one. "I like the dark wood," the young man said. "It makes the portrait look richer."

"I agree," said Warren.

"Did you pick out a mat?"

"I don't have a clue," answered Warren.

"Okay, I would suggest this one," as he placed the corner shaped mat sample at the inside corner of the frame up against the portrait.

"That looks good," said Warren. "Do it."

"Oh, you're lucky! That frame is twenty-five percent off the regular price. So it's only $58 for the frame. The mat is $30 because it's a specialty mat. The framing labor will be $100." He entered the three amounts into the register plus the tax. "The total will be $205.57."

Warren choked. "I had no idea framing a picture would cost so much. When will it be done? I need it tonight."

"Oh, boy, I don't think we can do that, sir."

The petite red-headed girl had come back and looked at what had been chosen for the portrait. "Oh," she said, "that will be stunning. What beautiful grandchildren."

"He wants it by tonight, but I don't think I can get to it."

"Nonsense," she said. "If you need it by tonight, we'll get it done," she promised Warren.

"Okay," said the young man, giving his co-worker a look, "she's the boss."

"Thank you so much," gushed Warren. "You are so kind. This is really important to me. I'll be back before 6 p.m."

****

Warren drove into Cecil's garage and shut the door just as Janet pulled onto the street.

Chapter 28

You Were Hard to Find

"Linda," her father said as he pulled her into the formal living room.

"Dad, what are you doing?"

"I need to talk to you and I don't want your mother to hear."

"Okay, okay, what's up?"

"I need you to do a really big favor for me and take your mother out tonight. I have to go out and I don't want her to know. She always gives me the third degree if I don't tell her where I'm going and I don't want to lie to her."

"Where are you going?" Linda asked with a suspicious look on her face.

"Promise not to tell you mother?"

"Dad, you're acting so mysterious. What are you up to?"

"I think I've found Laura Blaine, the children's mother."

"Wait. What?" Linda said too loud.

"Shhhh," hushed Warren. "Your mother will hear."

"How did you find her?"

"It was something Shawn said once when we were at a baseball game. I don't have time to go into details. I need to leave before 5:30. Where does your mother keep the pictures we took of the children?"

"She put them with the old family albums."

"And where is that?" he asked.

"Dad, you don't know where the family albums are? She keeps them in the bookcase in the family room."

Warren followed Linda into the kitchen. Janet had started to prepare dinner. "Hey, Mom, do you want to go to a movie tonight?" ask Linda.

"How sweet of you to ask, but I've been out all day with the quilters guild and I'll be too tired after I fix dinner and clean up. And…it looks like your father didn't wash the breakfast dishes." Janet went to the pantry to get some potatoes.

Linda gave her father a 'what do I do now look.' He mouthed, "Ask her out to dinner."

Janet came out of the pantry. "I don't have any potatoes."

"Mom, we can go out for dinner and let someone else cook the potatoes."

"I think that's a great idea. How often do you get to go out for dinner and a movie with your baby daughter?" said Warren. "I promise I will clean up the dishes."

"I guess you're right, but what will you eat for dinner?"

"I'll just fix a sandwich," he said.

"You had a sandwich for lunch."

"So I'll have one for dinner."

As soon as Linda and Janet left, Warren headed for the bookcase. He didn't see the pictures so he started to thumb through the albums looking between the pages. The third album was an older looking one and when he got to about the fifth page he saw a picture that hit him like a ton of bricks. He pulled it from the album and put it in his shirt pocket. He finally found the pictures he was looking for. They were still in the processing envelope. He took the ones he wanted and put the rest back very neatly so Janet wouldn't notice that anyone had been looking at the albums.

****

Warren went straight to the frame shop. The little red-headed girl saw him when he came in. She smiled at him and said, "I'll be right back. I think you're going to like it." She disappeared into the back area of the shop and came out with the framed portrait.

It took Warren's breath away. He just stood there and looked at it. To his surprise, tears started to well in his eyes. "Oh, my," he said, "that is absolutely beautiful. You did such a good job."

"I thought you would like it," she beamed. "Let me wrap it up for you." She again disappeared into the back.

****

Warren entered the Hardy Burger clinging to the wrapped portrait. He spotted a booth at the back, sat down, and put the portrait on the seat next to him. He was so nervous that he could scarcely breathe. A tall middle-aged woman with the name tag 'Carol' came over and plopped down a glass of water and asked, "What's your fancy today?"

Warren thought the name Carol didn't quite fit her. She looked like she could take on a linebacker. "Hi, Carol," he said.

"I'm not Carol," she shot back.

"Your name tag says you're Carol."

"It's not my tag, I borrowed it.

"Is Laura Blaine here?" he asked cautiously.

"Hey, Laura," she bellowed, "Some guy wants to see you!"

"Okay, thanks," came a voice from behind the counter. Warren was relieved that Not-Carol was also not Laura Blaine.

"So now what do you want to eat?" not-Carol asked again.

"I will have one of your famous Superburgers."

"To drink," she demanded.

Warren grabbed his water. "Water will be fine."

"Suit yourself," and she walked away.

Warren sipped on his water trying to calm his nerves, all the while watching Laura. She looked like a grown-up Kimber. She was very friendly and chatty with the customers. She didn't have the sparkle in her eyes like Kimber. Her eyes looked tired. He would look away when she turned his direction. He didn't want her to see him staring.

Not-Carol placed the Superburger in front of him. It was on a large plate with a big pile of French fries.

"Wow, that's a huge hamburger!" Warren exclaimed.

"That's why we call it a Superburger. Here's you bill," as she slapped it on the table. "You pay at the register up front."

He struggled to get his mouth around the Superburger and some sauce dripped on his shirt. He tried to wipe it off with a napkin. *Now Laura is going to think I'm a slob*, he thought. It was the best hamburger he had ever tasted but he didn't have much of an appetite because his stomach was in knots from nerves. He nibbled on French fries, still watching Laura. Just as he thought she had forgotten; she started to walk his way. He quickly looked down and pretended he was going to take another bite of hamburger.

"You wanted to see me?" Laura asked, in a soft voice.

Warren stood up and looked into her eyes. "Kimber," he said under his breath.

"What?" ask Laura.

"Oh, you look so much like Kimber."

Laura gave him a puzzled look. She did not recognize this man. "How do you know Kimber?"

"I'm sorry. I'm Warren Chapman." He stuck his hand out to offer a hand shake. "You were hard to find."

Her face changed from puzzled to shocked. She did not offer her hand back. "You were not supposed to find me."

"Laura," said Warren. "Can I call you Laura?"

"No, you can't call me Laura… or anything else."

"Please, won't you sit down?" pleaded Warren.

"No, can't you see I'm working?"

"Laura," a loud man's voice came from between the swinging doors, "take your break now while it has slowed down a little."

"Please sit," Warren pleaded again. Laura reluctantly sat down opposite Warren. "My wife and I missed the children and we wanted to know if they could come visit us once in a while."

"*No*," said Laura. "That is impossible," and she started to get up.

"Wait a minute," he said, "I want to show you something." He pushed the Superburger aside and placed the wrapped portrait on the table. Laura looked at it but didn't make a move.

"Go ahead, open it. I think you will like it."

"Mr. Chapman, you can't bribe me with a gift." She started to get up again.

Warren was losing his patience with this unreasonable woman. "Sit down," he barked. Laura sat down, shocked at his tone. "You left your children on our doorstep without a word and picked them up without a word. We fell in love with your children and you yanked them away from us." He ripped the wrapping away from the portrait and lifted it up in front of her face. She had no choice but to look at the portrait. Her face softened as she looked at each one of her children. Tears welled up in her eyes.

"My children," she gasped.

Not-Carol had heard Warren command Laura to sit down and she was concerned about how gruff he sounded. She was now standing at the booth ready to defend Laura. She saw the tears in Laura's eyes and said, "Laura, is this man bothering you?"

Not-Carol's question broke Laura out of her trance. She got up and shrieked at Warren. "You can't see my children; they are not your children. They are my children!" and she disappeared through the swinging doors.

Not-Carol barked "Mister, you had better leave before I call the cops. And if you come back I *will* call the cops."

"I'll leave," he said, feeling defeated. He put a twenty-dollar bill on the table.

"Hey mister, your picture."

Warren didn't answer and left Hardy Burger without the portrait.

He pulled the car into the garage and walked into the kitchen and there they were waiting for him—the breakfast dishes.

Chapter 29

I Want My Grandpa

Laura could feel one of her migraine headaches coming on. Not-Carol found Laura in the Hardy Burger kitchen and told her the rude man had left a large picture on the table and she handed it to Laura. "Are those your children?"

"Yes."

"Wow, you never told me you had such beautiful children."

Laura managed a 'thank you' and put the portrait in the manager's office. She had a very difficult time finishing her shift at the Hardy Burger. When she got home she put the portrait under her bed so the children wouldn't see it. They were all asleep, so she kissed each one, took a migraine headache pill, and went to bed.

Before she fell asleep, she thought about how the children had pleaded with her to let them visit the Chapmans and she always said 'no.' She was becoming very weary of Andrew constantly repeating, "I

159

want my Grandpa," and that was all he had said since he'd been home. She had asked him several times to stop, but he just looked at her with a defiant look on his face and said, "*I want my grandpa!*"

The first Monday morning when Laura dropped him off, Mrs. Sanders said, "Andrew, you've gained some weight! You look so much better." Andrew smiled at her. "And he smiles now! That vacation must have done a world of good for you, Andrew," she said.

"*I want my grandpa!*" he said as he walked into Mrs. Sander's house.

"Oh, my, and he talks, too; how wonderful," beamed Mrs. Sanders.

On Monday when Dawn picked up Andrew from Mrs. Sanders, the first thing Mrs. Sanders said was, "Can you get Andrew to stop with that constant chant, 'I want my grandpa?'" I think it was better when he didn't talk. Can you do something to make him stop? Who is this grandpa anyway? You never mentioned there were grandparents."

"I'm sorry about the chanting; we can't get him to stop either," Dawn said.

✳✳✳✳✳✳✳✳✳✳✳✳

"Dawn, I can't wake Mommy up. I shook her and called her name but she just lays there with her mouth open. She looks like she dead," Kimber said, melodramatically holding her arms up and letting them down gracefully.

"Oh, Kimber, don't be so dramatic."

Dawn went into the bathroom, turned on the hot water, and soaked a washcloth in warm water. She rung it out and headed for her mother's bedroom. She shook her mother and put the warm washcloth on her mother's face. The warmth of the washcloth brought Laura out of her sleep.

Laura rubbed her face with the washcloth. "Thanks, Dawn. What time is it?"

160

"Eleven o'clock," Dawn answered. "Mom, do you have one of your headaches?"

"Yes, it started last night. I'll get up in a minute."

About an hour later Laura came out in her bathrobe with wet hair. "Mom," said Dawn, "don't you have to go to work?"

"No, I called in sick earlier. I thought we could go shopping for school clothes today because you don't have school today."

"That means I'll be stuck with Andrew," Shawn complained.

"Do we have to go to a thrift store?" Dawn asked.

"Yes, we do. You know I can't afford anything else. Kimber, we can get you another ballet outfit," said Laura, trying to sound cheerful.

"I have a very nice ballet outfit at Grandma's house," she told her mother.

"Mother, Mrs. Chapman bought us all new clothes and I want to wear those clothes to school, not hand-me-downs," Dawn said.

"*I want my grandpa! I want my grandpa!*" Andrew started his chant.

"That's all I've heard since you children have been home. 'Grandpa this and Grandma that. Grandpa took me to the baseball game. Grandma makes great cookies. Grandma took me to ballet lessons.' You keep going on and on about the Chapmans. I'm sick of it!" Laura exploded. "I'm very glad you had such a wonderful time at the Chapmans but I have had enough of how the Chapmans did all those things for you. I can do only what I can do and that means going to the thrift store. You don't seem to remember the rules of the game you begged me to play. You signed a contract and promised to always follow the rules. You are not following the rules."

"*I want my grandpa! I want my grandpa! I want my grandpa!*"

"Andrew, would you stop that chanting!" Laura screamed at him. "You're driving me crazy and you are driving Mrs. Sanders crazy, too. She told me if you don't stop, I'll have to find someone else to watch you. I've had enough. I hate my life!" Laura screamed. She turned, went into her bedroom and slammed the door.

Both Kimber and Andrew were crying. Dawn and Shawn looked at each other, not knowing what to say. They had never seen their mother like this before.

"I have an idea," said Shawn. "Dawn, would you and Kimber make a picnic lunch? We can take Andrew to the park."

After the children had enjoyed the picnic lunch, Dawn and Shawn were sitting on a park bench watching Kimber and Andrew play on the jungle gym.

"You know, Shawn," said Dawn. "That was a very good idea you had to come and have a picnic in the park."

"Thanks, Dawn." He had to cherish the moment because she rarely gave him a compliment.

He said in return, "That was a really good picnic lunch. Better than the cheese sandwiches with those red things Grandma made." They both smiled remembering the Apple Hill trip. Shawn's face grew serious. "We need to talk about what happened with Mom."

"I know," Dawn agreed. "She's right. We haven't been following the rules. We helped make the rules and made a promise we would never break them."

He nodded in agreement and added, "She hasn't broken any of the rules. What are we going to do to make her feel better?"

"One of the rules was to not go back and visit the grandparents," said Dawn. "We wanted to break that rule the very first night."

"It was easy to keep that rule the first two times because I think the grandparents were glad to see us go," said Shawn. "But the Chapmans seemed to really love us."

"I miss Grandma so much," Dawn said softly, with longing in her voice.

"And I miss going to the baseball games with Grandpa."

"We're just going to have to get over wanting to visit the Chapmans," said Dawn. "You and I can rein ourselves in, but what about Kimber and Andrew? Kimber was really frightened when Mom yelled at us, and so was Andrew. I think Kimber won't say any more about the Chapmans if I make her promise. But Andrew may be a problem."

"I'll try to handle Andrew," volunteered Shawn.

"Okay, we have that problem worked out, but we need to find a way to apologize to her," said Dawn. They both sat there on the park bench in their own thoughts.

Shawn broke the silence with a question to his sister. "Do you think you can remember how to make those meatballs over rice thing Grandma made?"

"You mean the Lazy Dazy Meatballs?"

"Whatever they were, they were good," he replied, licking his lips.

"Yeah, I think I can, and I can also make the yummy garlic bread."

"Maybe you and Kimber can make that dinner and we can surprise Mom? I'll keep Andrew entertained."

Beaming at her brother, Dawn said, "That's an awesome idea." She shook her head with a big smile on her face. "I can't believe it! You had two great ideas in one day!"

****

"Dinner's ready" announced Dawn. "Kimber, would you go wake Mom, please?"

"No," said, Kimber, "I'm afraid."

"Okay, you finish setting the table and I'll wake her." Dawn opened the bedroom door slowly and peaked in the room. Her mother was combing her hair and saw Dawn's reflection in the mirror and smiled at her daughter. "Do you feel better, Mom?" asked Dawn.

"Yes, thanks. My headache is finally gone. What smells so good?"

"Kimber and I made dinner for you," Dawn said proudly. "It was Shawn's idea."

"Oh, that's so nice," said Laura with a lump in her throat.

Kimber, Shawn, and Andrew were sitting at the table waiting for Dawn and their mother. When Laura was settled into her chair she looked at each one of her children. "I'm so sorry for the way I acted earlier today. I lost my temper and it was a very unsuitable way for a mother to act." Tears were running down her face. "I promise it won't happen again."

"We're sorry, too, Mommy," said Dawn. "We promise we won't break the rules of the game anymore." They all took each other's hands and bowed their heads. Laura said the blessing on the food. She struggled to keep her emotions while thanking Heavenly Father for giving her such wonderful children and she asked Him to help her control her temper.

The little family helped themselves to the Lazy Dazy Meatballs over rice, garlic bread, corn, and a green salad.

"Dawn, this dinner is wonderful! Where did you learn how to make these tasty meatballs?" Laura asked.

Dawn looked at her mother but didn't answer. Laura understood and smiled at Dawn and Kimber.

Chapter 30

Second Try

Warren was very quiet during breakfast and Linda could tell things hadn't gone well with Laura Blaine. After breakfast, Linda cornered her father while Janet was doing the dishes. "What happened?" she questioned her father. "You look depressed."

"It didn't go very well. She was so unreasonable. She thinks we're trying to *steal* her children."

"That ungrateful woman! And after all you and Mom did for them so she could go on vacation… What are you going to do now?"

"Nothing. There's nothing I can do. She made it very clear she doesn't want us to see the children ever again."

"Dad, Dad, you can't give up. Just look at Mother. She mopes around and all she talked about last night was the kids. She fell in love with them and talked about how Andrew loves you. Just look at you Dad; you're not a happy camper. I've never known you to give up. You just go back there and try again. I'll go with you if you want. I rather like those kids myself. We can tell Mom that you and I are going to have a father-daughter night."

Warren perked up a little. "I'll think about it. Let's let things calm down and maybe we can go next week?"

✱✱✱✱✱✱✱✱✱✱✱✱

"What movie are you going to see?" asked Janet.

"I don't know," said, Warren. "We'll decide when we get to the theater."

"Have fun, you two," Janet called after them as they got into the car.

Linda said without thinking, "Here we go laughing and scratching." Father and daughter looked at each other smiling.

✱✱✱✱✱✱✱✱✱✱✱✱

They walked into the Hardy Burger and ran into Not-Carol, but her nametag said "Lee" this time. Fortunately, she did not remember Warren. He told Linda that she was the one that said she would call the cops on him if he came back.

"I thought you said her name was Carol," said Linda.

"No, she had borrowed Carol's tag. I guess her name is Lee. She looks more like a Lee."

He saw Laura behind the counter and directed Linda to sit at the counter. Laura came over and placed two menus in front of Linda and Warren. "What would you like to drink?" she asked as she glanced up and saw Warren. "What are you doing here?"

"I came to apologize for being so short with you last week. I'm very sorry."

"I'll have a diet cola," Linda said.

"This is my daughter, Linda," said Warren. Laura gave her a quick glance and turned and walked away not saying a thing in response.

"I see what you mean, Daddy; she's a witch."

Laura returned with the diet cola and water for Warren. "Have you decided what you want?" she asked coldly. Warren and Linda gave their orders and Laura walked away without a word or a smile.

"If she treats all her customers like this, it's a wonder she ever gets any tips," said Linda

"I've seen her with other costumers and she's very friendly. It's just me she doesn't like."

They watched Laura smile and be friendly to other customers, but when she placed Warren and Linda's food down, she didn't look at them.

"Laura," said Warren, "we aren't trying to steal the children away from you. We just want them to come visit us once in a while. They have brought happiness into our lives and I think they were happy being with us. I have pictures of them while they were with us…" He showed the picture of Kimber at her ballet recital.

"You should have seen her. She was amazing and looked so adorable," said Linda.

"I know," said Laura coldly, "I did see her."

"You did?" Warren said in surprise. "Kimber didn't say anything about you being there."

"I was standing in the back and left right after she finished dancing."

"And then you came and snatched them away that night," snapped Linda.

Laura looked at her without expression or comment. Warren held up to Laura the picture of when they were all on TV at Apple Hill.

"I saw them on TV, too," said Laura.

Warren took a newspaper clipping out of an envelope. "Did you see this article of Shawn at the baseball game? He was the one millionth fan to enter the park."

Laura glanced at the clipping with surprise.

He handed it to her. "That was the night the game was played to honor all those that lost their lives serving our country. Your husband, Christian Blaine, has his name in the article." Laura's face softened a little. "Here are some other pictures of the children while they stayed with us. You can see how happy they were with us." He handed Laura the envelope with the pictures.

"I know my children were happy staying with you. They have told me several times. But they can't come back and stay with you again because it is against the rules of the game. They signed a contract," and she walked away with the envelope in her hand.

"The children talked about a game," said Linda. "What's up with that game?"

Warren was more focused on the other thing Laura said: the children told her they were happy when they stayed with him and Janet. "I think she has softened a little," said Warren. It gave him courage for the next step of his plan to get the children back.

While father and daughter ate, Laura completely ignored them. "Linda," said Warren, "see if you can get Laura's attention to come back over."

Linda gulped down her soda and called to Laura as she walked by to wait on another customer. "May I please have some more soda?" she asked very politely.

"I'll be there in a minute."

Warren looked at his daughter. "That was very impressive."

Laura took another customer's order and grabbed Linda's soda glass on her pass-by. Linda and Warren had finished eating their food by the time Laura came back with a new glass of soda.

"Mrs. Blaine, I have one more picture I want you to see."

Laura looked at him in disgust. "All right, I'll look at one more picture, but then I want you to leave me alone."

Warren took the picture out of the breast pocket of his shirt. He held it out to Laura. This picture wasn't like the others. It had scalloped edges and looked like it had been taken in a different era. Laura snatched the picture and looked down at it. As she studied the picture, a puzzled frown came to her face. "When did you take this picture of Dawn?"

"That is not a picture of Dawn; it's a picture of my wife when she was Dawn's age."

Laura tossed the picture down in front of Warren. Linda grabbed it to take a look for herself. "Oh, my, it does look like Dawn!"

Mrs. Blaine, you know the small purple, diamond-shaped birthmark Dawn has on the inside of her leftankle? My wife has the same identical birthmark."

"So," said Laura, "a lot of people have the same birthmark. My husband had one."

Don't you think it's strange that Dawn looks so much like my wife and they both have the same birthmark?" asked Warren.

"No," Laura said. "It's most likely a coincidence."

"What are you getting at, Dad?" Linda asked.

Warren didn't hear Linda. He could only think of the next question he was going to ask Laura. "Mrs. Blaine, was your husband adopted?"

Laura looked a Warren with disgusted shock. "No, he's not adopted. His parents live in Montana. Why would you ask that question?"

"Yes," added Linda, "the children told Mom and me their father's parents live in Montana on a cattle ranch." The two women looked at each other in agreement. "So why would you ask that, Dad?" Linda was just as puzzled as Laura.

"Well, because…" He turned to his daughter, but stopped mid-sentence. He had been so caught up in his plan that he hadn't realized Linda would hear what he was about to tell Laura. He and Janet had never shared the secret with their children. "Oh, nevermind," he said. "I think we've used up enough of Laura's time."

"No, Dad," demanded Linda, "I want to know why you asked that question."

"Come on, we had better go." And he started to get up from the counter.

Laura was curious with this sudden change of Warren's mood. She was happy to see him in the hot seat and not her.

Linda pushed her father back down onto the barstool. "I'm not leaving here until you tell me why you asked her if her husband was adopted," Linda demanded, glaring at her father.

Warren sat there with his head down not knowing exactly what to do. He knew if he didn't tell Linda she would hound him forever and maybe even talk to Janet about what he had just said. But if his theory was right and he didn't tell the secret now, he would never know. In a split second he decided to tell Linda the secret.

"You promise you will not tell your mother what I'm about to tell you?" he looked at Linda sternly.

"Daddy, you're scaring me."

"It's okay, sweetheart; we will tell your mother later."

Laura stood there with her mouth open, eager to hear the secret story. "Linda, you know how smart your mother is? She skipped a couple of grades in school. She graduated from high school when she was fifteen and a half and attended college at sixteen. She was very mature for her age and everyone thought she was older." He paused, searchig for just the right words.

"Is that it?" ask Linda.

"No, there's more," he said gently to his daughter. Laura had to lean in a little closer to hear. She didn't want to miss a word.

Warren took a deep breath. "Your mother met and fell in love with a young man. He was the brother of her best friend in college. He didn't know your mother was so young. He had joined the Air Force to become a fighter pilot. He asked Janet to marry him before he was sent to Air Force Flight Training. So they ran off to Reno and got married and didn't tell anyone. After he had been gone for three months, your mother realized she was pregnant."

Linda started at her father in bewilderment. "Mother was married before?"

"Yes, his name was Dale Douglas. She wrote him a letter telling him the news. He wrote back and told her he was working on getting leave so he could come and they would face her parents together. It took another month for his leave to be approved. The day before he was to leave for home, he was killed on a training mission."

"Oh, how sad," said Linda.

"Janet's parents were sitting on the front porch when two uniformed Air Force personnel approached them and asked to see Mrs. Dale Douglas. Of course, they didn't know a Mrs. Dale Douglas and told the uniformed men they must have the wrong address. The officers said that she is also known as Janet Smith. The Smiths were bewildered and Mrs. Smith went into the house to find Janet.

"When Janet came out one of the uniformed men asked her if she was Mrs. Dale Douglas. It was a very awkward moment but she confessed that she was. He handed her an official Air Force envelope and informed her that Dale had been killed. Your mother collapsed on the spot."

"Her parents were not happy with the situation, especially when they found out she was pregnant. They told her she was too young to be tied down with a baby and it would be best to give it up for adoption. She could continue in college without the responsibility of caring for a baby. They also added that most men do not want to marry a woman who already has a child.

"At first she refused. She told them the baby was the only thing she had left of Dale. After many tearful discussions with her parents and a couple of counselors, Janet decided it would be best for her baby to have two parents. With a broken heart, she gave up her precious baby boy with the little purple diamond-shaped birthmark on the inside of his left ankle. Mrs. Blaine, is your husband's birthday April 25, 1973?"

Laura's face paled, but she did not answer his question.

"Oh, my," said Linda. "Poor Mom." Linda sat there in silence thinking over the story her father just told her when the thought hit her. "So Daddy, you think that the baby boy mother gave away was Laura Blaine's husband?"

"Wait a minute," said Laura. "If you think I'm going to fall for that cockamamie story and act you two just put on, you are sadly mistaken. You guys are crazy. Mr. Chapman, if you ever try to talk to me again I will report you for harassment."

"Mrs. Blaine, if you accuse my father of harassment, I will call Social Services and report that you dumped your children on our doorstep and have you charged with child neglect," Linda shot back, defending her father. The two women glared at each other until Laura stomped off.

On the drive home Linda asked her father, "What are we going to do now?"

"I don't know. I only know I keep having this feeling that Laura Blaine's husband is your mother's baby boy. Let's wait a while before we tell your mother that I told you the secret. I think she will be very angry with me and I'm just too tired to handle it right now. And you know we will have to tell your brother and sister."

"I think they will be okay with it, Dad. We are all grown up now and we won't love her any less."

＊＊＊＊＊＊＊＊＊＊＊＊

"You two are home early. What happened?" asked Janet. They both forgot about the movie. Both of them were too emotionally drained.

"Oh, we just ate and forgot about the movie," said Linda.

"Where did you eat?" asked Janet.

"The Hardy Burger," answered Warren.

"The Hardy Burger!" exclaimed Janet. "Of all the places to eat, you ate *there*?"

Linda looked at her mother in a way she had never looked at her before and realized just how much she loved this woman who had raised her. She went over to her mother wrapped her arms around her and held her tight and said, "I love you very much, Mother," tears streaming down her face.

"Oh, my goodness what brought this on? I love you very much, too." She was hugging her daughter just as tight.

Chapter 31

Incredulous

Dawn shook her mother and said, "Mom, it's time to get up." Laura opened her eyes and squinted at the daylight. Dawn handed her mother a warm washcloth. "Mom, do you have one of your migraine headaches again?"

"Yes, I do," answered Laura placing the warm washcloth on her face.

"We've had breakfast and we're all ready for school. I'll take Andrew to Mrs. Sanders' and get her daughter. We will be ready for you to drive us to school," said Dawn.

"Thank you. You are the best daughter." Laura pulled on a pair of jeans and an oversized t-shirt. She brushed her hair and put on a dab of lipstick.

"Mommy, I'm sorry you have a headache," said Kimber.

"Thank you, sweetheart, I'm sorry, too. I haven't been the best mother lately."

"Mother," Dawn said gently, "did you forget it's Andrew's birthday today?

"Oh," moaned Laura, "I did forget his birthday. I'll just have to do something to make it up to him."

"Maybe we can have a party for him tonight," suggested Kimber, "while you are at work."

"I think that is a very nice idea," Laura replied.

"Are you going to your state job today?" asked Dawn.

"No, I think I'll call in sick and try to get rid of this headache."

"Maybe you could get him a birthday cake?" suggested Dawn.

"I'll do that. You children are so good." They each kissed her as they got out of the car, except Shawn. He patted his mother on the shoulder as he got out.

✶✶✶✶✶✶✶✶✶✶✶

Laura took another migraine headache pill and went back to bed. Her sleep was fitful; she kept having the same dream of Mr. Chapman and her husband, Christian.

Mr. Chapman was asking, "Is your husband adopted? Why do my wife and Dawn look so much alike? Why do my wife and Christian have the same birthmark?"

Christian was saying, "I knew my parents loved me. They gave me everything I needed while I was growing up, but somehow I didn't feel like I belonged to them. I didn't like the ranch. I wanted to be a soldier."

It was 2 p.m. when she finally got up. She still had the headache, but it was not so bad. She tried to eat, but the food just didn't taste good. She tried to watch TV, but images of her dream flooded her mind. What was it she always told her children when they had a problem? She got on her knees and poured her heart out to Heavenly Father. When she finished her prayer, she knew what to do.

Laura picked up the phone receiver and dialed the three prefix numbers and then quickly put the receiver back down. "I can't do this," she said out loud and walked away from the phone. The pain and confusion came back. "I have to know," she said aloud, "or I will never be at rest."

She kneeled down by the bed again and pleaded with her Heavenly Father to give her the courage to call. A peace came over her and she walked back to the phone. This time she dialed the number and waited while the phone rang. She counted six rings trying to keep up her courage. Just as she was ready to hang up, a polite but formal voice said, "Hello?" She knew that voice; it was her mother-in-law, Anne Blaine. Anne's husband, Robert, owned and operated a big cattle ranch in Montana. It had been his parent's ranch and Robert had worked very hard to build it up. Laura had always been a little frightened of Robert because he spoke his mind no matter who it hurt. Anne was pretty much under his control and Laura never really had a chance to get close to her.

"Hello? the voice said again, sounding irritated.

"Hello, Anne," said Laura letting her breath out. "This is Laura."

"Oh, Laura, how are you?" Anne said with a softer voice, but still formal.

"I'm fine," answered Laura.

"How are the children?" asked Anne with the same voice.

"They are just fine," said Laura. "I guess you're wondering why I called."

"Yes, it's a bit of a surprise to hear from you."

"I want to ask you a question and I don't quite know how except to come right out and ask it." She could hear her voice trembling.

"Okay, come out with it, what is it?"

Laura took a death breath, "Was Christian adopted?"

There was silence on the other end of the phone line. Laura waited, not knowing what else to say. Then she thought she heard what sounded like sniffling. "Anne, are you there?" Laura asked timidly.

"Oh, Laura, can you ever forgive me?" sobbed Anne.

Laura was stunned by this sudden change of Anne's mood. "Forgive you for what?"

"For ignoring you and the children. It wasn't my idea, it was Robert's. He was very hurt and angry at Christian for not wanting to stay in Montana and help with the cattle ranch. He couldn't understand why he joined the Air Force. He and Christian had a horrible fight about Christian making the Air Force his career and not the ranch. Christian packed his things and left that night. He would never visit and when he phoned, if his father answered, he would hang up. I pleaded with Christian to come home but he wouldn't because of his father. I just don't understand what happened. We loved him as if he was our own. And when Christian was killed it made Robert even angrier. What a waste of life, Robert would say.

Laura was shocked. She had never heard Anne ramble on like this. She had always been so cautious when she spoke.

"We were told we could never have children," continued Anne. "We were going to tell Christian he was adopted, but when I got pregnant with our daughter, Amy, we didn't want him to feel he wasn't wanted, so we never told him. Both Robert and I tried to pay more attention to Christian because he was adopted. But Amy demanded so much of our time and Robert adored her. He gave her anything she wanted. Maybe we paid too much attention to her because she was our own. I just don't know. Laura, I'm so sorry. Can you ever forgive me? I have been holding this guilt for so long."

"Anne," Laura said softly, "what you just told me explains a lot and I do forgive you. You and Robert did a wonderful job raising Christian. He was so good to our children. He must have learned that from you, Anne. I loved him so much."

"We loved him, too. But why did you ask me if Christian was adopted?"

"It's a long story," Laura said, stalling for time to think what she would tell Anne. It had not occurred to her to prepare for this question. "The children have been visiting one of my co-worker's parents, Warren and Janet Chapman. They have become very fond of the children." She decided not to tell Anne about The Family Game. "As it turns out, Dawn looks just like Janet Chapman when she was Dawn's age. In fact, when Warren Chapman showed me a picture of Janet, I thought it was a picture they had taken of Dawn. Janet also has a birthmark just like the one Christian had. Dawn has the same one. You know the little purple diamond on the inside of the left ankle."

"Yes," replied Anne.

"Janet ran off and married an Air Force pilot and became pregnant right away. He was killed when his plane went down on a training mission. Janet was only seventeen and her parents talked her into giving up her baby boy for adoption. It broke Janet's heart, but she believed it was the best thing to do. She married again and had three children, but she never forgot the baby boy she gave up. I know it sounds like a long shot, but Mr. Chapman believes that my children are his wife's grandchildren."

"As I think back now," said Anne, "Christian's birth mother was young and her husband had been killed. Laura, I think I still have the adoption papers packed away somewhere. It may take me awhile, but I think I can find them. If it is true that the children are this Janet Chapman's grandchildren, maybe by uniting them with her, I can make up for neglecting them. What is Janet's maiden name and her first married name?"

Chapter 32

That's Me

Laura's mind was racing after the conversation with Anne, but her headache was gone. She showered and got dressed. Now she was hungry. She fixed a baloney sandwich and something crinkled in her pants pocket when she sat down. It was the envelope Mr. Chapman had given her with the pictures of the children. She laid them out on the table and looked at them while eating. She picked up the picture of her children swimming in the Chapman's pool. She noticed there was a piece of paper stuck to the back of a picture. It was a note from Mr. Chapman.

"Dear Mrs. Blaine; I hope you see how happy your children are in these pictures. All we want to do is help you and have the children visit with us once in a while. If you change your mind, here is our phone number."

Her heart was burning now. She took a deep breath and walked to the phone.

"Hello, this is Warren," she heard on the other end of the phone line.

"Mr. Chapman, this is Laura Blaine." Warren held his breath and didn't know what to say.

"It's Andrew's birthday today. Would you like to come pick the children up and keep them for the weekend?" she asked.

Warren let out his breath and said, "Yes, we would really like that."

"The children will be home about 3:30. Can you be here at 4:30? We live in the Winnicutt Apartments off Winding Way at the end of Winnicutt Circle. It's apartment number 2."

"I'll be there, Mrs. Blaine and…thank you." He hung up the phone, threw his arms in the air, and shouted, "Hurray, hurray!" But his elation was short lived…Janet was gone with the car.

****

Laura walked to Mrs. Sanders' house right next to their apartment. Mrs. Sanders answered the door and said, "Oh, hi, Laura. This is a surprise. Did you get off work early today?" Laura ignored the question and said, "I would like to take Andrew home now."

"Alright," said Mrs. Sanders. "Is everything, okay?"

"Everything is fine."

"I'm worried about Andrew. He doesn't chant anymore, but he is not a happy boy. I can't get him to eat and he has that sad look on his face again," said Mrs. Sanders.

"I know," sighed Laura, "but that's going to change tonight." Andrew saw his mother through the open door and came to her. "Mrs. Sanders, thanks so much for all you do for Andrew. Come on, Andrew, I have a big surprise for your birthday." Andrew just kept walking and didn't acknowledge his mother.

When they got home, she sat him in a chair and said, "Sit right here while I get your surprise." His eyes followed her as she took the thrift store picture off the wall and let it fall down behind the sofa. He watched as she disappeared into the bedroom and came out with the portrait of the children. She hung it on the wall over the sofa. Andrew stared at the portrait a while. He jumped off the chair, ran over to the sofa, and stood up on it. He pointed at himself and said, "That's me."

"Yes, it is," said Laura, as she sat down on the sofa. "Come down here and sit with me. I have another surprise to tell you." He flopped down on the sofa next to her. "Your Grandpa Chapman is coming to get you and your sisters and Shawn. Would you like to spend the weekend with your Grandma and Grandpa?"

Andrew's eyes lit up; he energetically nodded his head and smiled. What a different little boy he was in just a few seconds! She wished she could make him so happy. He threw himself at her, put his little arms around her neck, and almost choked her with his hug. *Well, maybe it is me that is making him happy,* she thought. "Are you hungry?" she asked. He again nodded his head 'yes.' She showed him the pictures Mr. Chapman had given her while he ate his baloney sandwich.

****

"The other children will be home soon, so let it be our little secret. We'll let them find the big picture themselves."

He nodded 'yes' and smiled mischievously.

Shawn came in first. "I'm hungry. What's to eat?"

Kimber walked in next and with a cheery voice said, "Happy birthday, Andrew."

He said, "Okay," and looked at his mother with a grin. She grinned back.

Dawn came into the kitchen just in time to see her mother's and Andrew's grins. "What's all the grinning about?" she asked.

"You'll see," her mother said.

"Does it have to do with Andrew's birthday?" Dawn asked her mother.

Andrew was grinning ear-to-ear, clapping his hands. "I guess it does. It must be good because I haven't seen him this happy since we were with the Chap…," she stopped mid-sentence.

Shawn was eating a baloney sandwich and Kimber was singing "Happy Birthday" to Andrew when they heard a squeal from Dawn. Dawn was looking at the portrait. "Mother, where did you get this?"

"Mr. Chapman gave it to me."

"You've seen Grandpa!" Shawn said with a month full of bread and boloney.

"Yes, he's been bugging me to let you children visit them." The rest of the family joined Dawn to look at the portrait. "Shawn, you look so handsome—just like your father. Dawn, you and Kimber look so pretty. The Chapman's must have spent a fortune on those beautiful dresses. And just look at Andrew. He is so adorable. It's an awesome picture of all of you," Laura said with a lump in her throat.

"Mommy there," announced Andrew.

"What did you say, Andrew?" asked Dawn.

"Mommy was there," he said again, this time a little louder.

"What do you mean 'Mommy was there'?" Shawn asked.

"I was there at Mrs. Archer's," confessed Laura.

The other three children looked at their mother with puzzled faces. "How could you be there?" questioned Shawn. "You were at a wonderful vacation resort."

"Mrs. Archer's house is almost like a wonderful vacation resort."

"Ooooh," said Dawn, "the peacock, the staircase, the library, the dining room. All those things you described are from Mrs. Archer's house."

"Yes, I have to admit they are," confessed Laura.

Dawn gave her brother a look and said, "I told you so."

"Man, you looked just like Grandma when you said that," Shawn shot back at her.

"You know what else?" said Laura, "I saw you on TV and I also watched Kimber dance at her recital. Kimber, you were so magnificent. You looked just like a perfect ballerina." She put her arm around Kimber and kissed her on the forehead.

"Grandpa coming," announced Andrew.

The other children looked at Andrew and then at their mother with hopeful looks on their faces.

"Yes, he's coming to take you for the weekend," she smiled at them. "So you'd better hurry and get packed." They all gave their mother a quick hug and scurried off to pack.

Chapter 33

Janet, You're a Genius

Janet had told Warren where she was going but, like so many times before, he just let it go in one ear and out the other. Now Warren was racking his brain trying to think where Janet had gone and when she would be back. He decided to call Linda; maybe she would know. He dialed her cell phone and got her voice message. "Linda," said Warren with urgency, "call me." The phone rang as soon as he put the receiver down.

"Hello, this is Warren," with urgency still in his voice.

"Dad, Dad, what is it?" said Linda. "I couldn't get to my phone before the voice mail picked it up. Is everything alright?"

He didn't answer her. "Where's your mother?"

"I don't know. I'm in New York. What's going on? Why don't you know where Mother is?" She was sounding frightened now.

"She left with the car and I need the car."

"Is that all it is—you need the car?" chuckled, Linda. "Maybe she went shopping."

"Oh, that's right, I remember, she said she wanted to buy something on sale and would be right back. I'm sorry I bothered you, Linda. Thanks! Bye!"

"Wait a minute, wait a minute! Why is it so important that you need the car? You sound like it's life or death."

"Laura Blaine called and said we could have the children for the weekend. She also told me her husband, Christian, was adopted."

"Oh my, oh my! That's great! Does Mom know?

"No, I want to surprise her. I think I hear the garage door opening. I'd better go. Bye."

He met Janet just as she was coming into the kitchen from the garage. "I'm so glad to see you."

It took Janet by surprise. He looked so exuberant; not like his grumpy self when she left him.

"I decided to do a little grocery shopping while I was out. There is another bag in car. Would you get it?" He rushed passed her and had the bag of groceries back before she could set the bag she was holding in the pantry.

"Janet," he yelled.

"Yes, Warren, I'm right here in the pantry."

"I have to go. I'll be back in about an hour."

"Where are you going in such a hurry?"

"Janet, I can't tell you. It's a surprise." He noticed the layer cake she had put on racks to cool while she was shopping. "You made a cake! Janet, you're a genius," he said with a big grin on his face. He hugged her and planted a big kiss on her lips.

Janet giggled, "Yes, I do make cakes on occasion. It must be some surprise because you are absolutely giddy."

"Janet, can you put three candles on the cake?" he said, on his way out the door. "And don't make dinner."

Janet was smiling while she put the groceries away. She was pleased to see Warren happy again. She thought, *"He must be having fun working on the surprise, but why does he want three candles on the cake? Candles are for someone having a birthday. I don't know anyone turning three. What a minute, I do know someone who is turning three. Andrew!* Her heart skipped a beat. *Has he found the children? Is he bringing them here? If he is, I need to get this cake frosted.* She was singing while she started on the cake. Then a thought hit her. *"What if I'm wrong and he's not bringing the children? What if the three candles mean something else? He didn't say it was a birthday cake. He hasn't said anything about even looking for the children after that disaster at the school. If he isn't bringing the children I will be so disappointed. I need to get a grip and not expect that the children are coming. I need to act happy no matter what he surprises me with. He seems so happy and I don't want to change that."* She wasn't singing anymore.

✳✳✳✳✳✳✳✳✳✳✳

The children were all standing out by the carport with their suitcases when Warren drove up. They waved at him with excitement. He felt his heart swell. They looked so happy to see him. When he got out of the car all the children rushed him and gave him a group hug.

"Go ahead and get in the car. I want to talk with your mother a minute." Laura was standing a little ways off watching the happy reunion.

"Thank you again, Mrs. Blaine," he said. Laura managed a smile. "How did you find out your husband was adopted?"

"His mother told me. She is trying to find the adoption papers to see if there is any information about your wife. I told her your wife's first married name was Janet Douglas. Is that right?"

He nodded and said, "Yes. Would you like to come to our home for dinner on Sunday? I know Janet would like to meet you."

"I don't know. I'll call you if that's okay," she answered.

Warren got in the car and the children all waved and threw kisses at their mother except for Shawn. It was too mushy for him.

"What did you and my mother talk about?" asked Dawn.

"I asked her if she would like to come for dinner on Sunday and she said she would think about it."

Laura watched as Warren drove away with her children. She was gripped with a sad loneliness. She had mixed feelings about the situation. She was happy they were happy, but she felt she was losing them. First she lost her parents, then her husband, and now her children. She got in her car and drove to the cemetery to put flowers on Christian's grave.

Chapter 34

Tradition

As Warren drove away he said, "We're going to stop and order some pizza. And while the pizza is cooking we'll go to the store and get stuff for salad and root beer floats.

"Oh, goody, that's our tradition dinner!" Kimber squealed.

"Grandma doesn't know you're coming. It will be a big surprise."

"I remember the first night we had the tradition dinner," said Dawn. "It was so nice."

"Are we going to get that same pizza? It was good pizza." Shawn was smacking his lips.

"We are getting the exact everything; it is tradition," Warren declared.

"Tradition," echoed Andrew.

"Was that Andrew I just heard?" asked Warren.

"Yes, it was," answered Shawn.

"Grandpa," said Dawn, "do you want to know the first thing he ever said? It was '*I want my grandpa*,' and he said it over, and over, and over. He chanted it for a week until Mom made him stop. He drove everyone crazy with it."

"So, Andrew," said Warren. "I see you missed me as much as I missed you."

"If it's a surprise, can we add flowers?" asked Kimber.

"I think that's a wonderful idea," answered Warren.

✱✱✱✱✱✱✱✱✱✱✱✱

Warren drove the car into the garage "Are we all ready? Let's do our check list." Sounding official, he said. "Shawn?"

"Pizza!" answered Shawn.

"Dawn?"

"Salad stuff!" answered Dawn.

"Kimber?"

"Ice cream!" answered Kimber.

"Grandpa?" said Warren. "Rootbeer!" he responded. "Andrew?"

"Flowers!" answered Andrew. They all piled out of the car giggling.

Janet had her head in the refrigerator rearranging things with her nervous energy, waiting for her surprise. She had her back to the garage door that led into the kitchen.

Andrew came in first. "Hi, Grandma," he said.

She turned around and there was Andrew holding out a bunch of flowers. She fell to her knees, with instant tears filling her eyes and she gave him a big hug. Then she realized he talked. "You talked," she said, smiling through her tears. All the others had gathered behind Andrew. She looked at them adoringly. "This is the best surprise ever." Warren helped his wife up from the floor and she hugged each child and Warren.

There was a flurry of conversation at the dinner table. The children talked about how much they missed Grandma and Grandpa. They told how they had been begging their mother to let them come visit, but she always said 'no.' They described how their mom made Andrew stop repeating, "*I want my grandpa*," and how he stopped talking again. But on Andrew's birthday everything changed.

"I think it was Andrew who changed her mind," said Kimber. "Because she knew he would never be happy for the rest of his life."

"No," argued Dawn, "I think it was the portrait Grandpa gave her."

"Whatever it was, I'm just glad she changed her mind," said Shawn. "This pizza is great," as he helped himself to a fourth piece.

"Mommy saw me dance at my ballet recital," said Kimber, "and she saw us on TV!"

"When we were at Mrs. Archer's house, she was there, too," said Dawn.

"What?" said Janet. "How do you know?"

"Andrew saw her. Remember when we were in the library waiting for Mrs. Archer and Andrew ran behind the sofa?"

"Yes," said Janet.

"Well, she was hiding behind the sofa," said Dawn. "She didn't want anyone to see her so she ducked behind the sofa before we came into the library. She didn't know it was us until we started talking. Because Andrew wasn't talking then, we didn't find out until today, just before Grandpa came to get us."

Warren laughed and said, "That's very funny that she was hiding behind the sofa. It was lucky for her Andrew didn't talk."

"She watched us eat dinner until Mrs. Bean caught her," continued Dawn. "And she even played with Andrew in the game room."

"Why was your mother at Mrs. Archer's?" asked Janet.

"She worked as her personal assistant while the regular one was on vacation," answered Dawn.

"All the time we thought she was on a great vacation, she was working for Mrs. Archer," added Shawn.

Warren told his story of how he found their mother. "Grandma and I almost got arrested for hanging out by the public school near Mrs. Archer's house."

"We don't go to public school. We go to a private school. That's why Mom works the second job. To pay for the private school," said Dawn.

Sounding a little miffed, Janet said, "Grandpa didn't tell me he knew your last name before April told us."

"I promised Shawn I wouldn't tell, and we men need to stick together. Besides what did it matter then? We didn't want to find their mother because we were having too much fun with the children."

"Grandpa, how did you find my mommy?" asked Kimber.

"It was something Shawn said about Superburgers. I heard a commercial on TV about Superburgers and I found your mother at the Hardy Burger. Janet," he turned to his wife. "You don't know what kind of hassle I went through to get the portrait printed and framed in one day."

"You got the portrait printed and framed in one day? That's incredible and must have been some kind of miracle!" Janet exclaimed.

"We love the portrait," said Dawn.

"Anyway," continued Warren "I gave your mother the portrait, but she still wouldn't let you children come visit us. Linda talked me into going to see your mother the second time. She missed all of you, too."

"I love Linda," said Kimber with a smile.

"Warren, when did you do all this visiting with the children's mother?" asked Janet.

"The first time you had dinner with Linda, and Linda went with me the second time."

"Why didn't you ask me to go with you instead of Linda?" Janet demanded.

"I didn't want you to get your hopes up and then have your heart broken again. Besides, didn't you like being surprised?"

"Yes, this has been a wonderful surprise," she said as she smiled at all the children.

"Surprise!" said Andrew.

"Talking about surprises, I'm so happy you are talking now," Janet said to Andrew. "So we better start celebrating your birthday. How old are you?"

"I'm three," and he held up four fingers.

Warren lit the candles on the birthday cake and everyone sang "Happy Birthday." Andrew even sang to himself, clapping, and smiling ear to ear.

"I know I must look like a Weepy Wanda, but I can't help but cry again. This is just so wonderful, all of us being together again," said Janet.

Chapter 35

The Phone Call

The ringing phone woke Laura from a sound sleep. She looked at the clock; it was 10:30 a.m. She couldn't believe she had slept so late. Shaking her head and taking a deep breath, she answered the phone trying not to sound sleepy.

"Laura, this is Anne. I searched until late last night trying to find the adoption papers. I just can't remember where I put them. The only thing I can think of is maybe they are in Robert's office safe. He's the only one who knows the combination. I'm sorry," said Anne.

"Thanks for trying," answered Laura.

"But the good news is we may not need them!" Anne said with enthusiasm. The strangest thing happened when the mailman delivered the mail. There was a letter addressed to Janet Douglas with our address. The letter is postmarked 1973 and it's from a Sacramento adoption agency."

"That *is* strange," agreed Laura.

"I would have sent it back to the post office except for you telling me about Janet Chapman. I just wonder why it took so long to be delivered. And why does Janet Douglas' mail have our address?"

"Maybe someone at the adoption agency made a clerical error and put the wrong address on the letter. Maybe it was delivered in 1973 and at that time you didn't know who Janet Douglas was so you probably sent it back. Maybe the post office decided to clean out the dead letter files and redeliver all the mail."

Anne took in all of what Laura said. "You know, I bet that's exactly what happened."

"Did you open the letter?"

"No, I didn't. It doesn't belong to me; it belongs to Janet Douglas," surprised that Laura would ask her such a question.

"Would you overnight it to me?" Laura asked. "I would like to give it to Janet."

"I'll do better than that. I will have Robert's personal courier fly to Sacramento and deliver it to you."

"Are you sure, Anne? I don't want to get you in trouble," replied Laura.

"All these years I have been afraid of what Robert would think if I did something he didn't like. But this ranch is half mine, so I think I can use his courier. Call me and let me know what's in the letter?"

"Of course I will," Laura said affectionately. "And thank you, Anne."

In the short time she had talked with Anne on the phone, she had grown fond of her. She was a different Anne; not like the one who put on an act for the benefit of her husband, Robert Blaine. But what puzzled Laura, was why Anne was so willing to prove that Janet Chapman was the birth mother of her son? Laura wondered why she was working so hard at it herself when she really didn't want to share the children? She did know that when she refused to let her children see the Chapmans they were very unhappy. And she knew when she decided to call Anne she felt relief from her anguish.

****

For several reasons, Laura decided not to go to church. She was anxious to get the letter from Anne and she just wasn't ready to respond to the questions she'd get about where the children were. She needed to find out if her husband was Janet Chapman's son.

Laura was reading the scriptures when there was a knock at the door. "Laura Blaine?" asked a tall man holding an envelope.

"Yes, I'm Laura Blaine."

"I'm Mr. Robert Blaine's courier and Mrs. Blaine sent this."

"Thank you so much," said Laura as she took the envelope.

****

Laura called the Chapmans and Janet answered the phone. Laura was very nervous; she was hoping that Warren would have answered. She wasn't sure she was ready to talk with Janet.

Hello, this is Laura Blaine," she said hesitantly.

Janet was just as apprehensive to talk to Laura, but said. "I hope you'll come for dinner tonight. I would love to meet you. We'll be eating dinner at five." Janet had decided that no matter how she felt about Laura Blaine, she needed to make friends with her, especially if they were going to share the children.

Laura was not sure she could handle spending a whole evening sharing her children with the Chapmans. After a brief pause, she responded, "I won't be coming for dinner. I'll just be by to pick the children up at 6:30. I have something I want to give you."

"Of course. That will be fine. I'll have them ready and thank you so much for letting them stay with us. We've enjoyed them so much." Janet wondered what on earth Laura Blaine could have for her…

Chapter 36

The Letter

Laura rang the doorbell at the Chapmans' house. She thought back to when her children rang the same doorbell. She wondered if they were as nervous as she was right now. To her relief, Warren answered the door. His warm welcome put her a little at ease but she still had tons of butterflies in her stomach. He led her into the kitchen where her three oldest children were helping with the dishes. Andrew saw his mother and ran to her. She kneeled down and gave him a hug. "Hi, Mommy," he said. "I'm having fun." Little did Andrew know how much that hug meant to her. The other children all said 'hi' and Kimber threw her a kiss.

Janet wiped her hands on the apron she was wearing as she walked over to Laura and extended her hand. "I'm Janet Chapman and I'm so glad to meet you."

Laura took Janet's hand and said, "I'm happy to meet you, too," even though she wasn't sure she really meant it. Laura was never good with small talk so she got right to the point and asked Janet "Is there somewhere we could be alone?"

Janet smiled and motioned for Laura to follow her into the front room. She invited Laura to sit in an armchair and she sat on the sofa. Janet was a little anxious about what Laura was going to give her because she wasn't sure what to think of this woman.

"First of all, I want to thank you and Mr. Chapman for treating my children so kindly and for all the things you've done for them. I know you must think I'm a terrible mother for just dropping them off, but it was what the children wanted. They made up this Family Game and it had very strict rules. But that's not what I want to talk about now; maybe some other evening when the children can help tell you and Mr. Chapman about the game if they haven't already told you."

"I know there is a game but they haven't explained it to Warren and me."

"I guess you know their father was killed in the war?" Janet nodded 'yes.' "He was a wonderful husband and father, Mrs. Chapman. You would have loved him." Tears filled Laura's eyes and were starting to spill onto her cheeks.

"Call me Janet," Janet said softly with compassion and she handed Laura a tissue box. Laura dabbed at the tears on her face.

"As I was saying, you would have loved him," and she took Janet's hand in both of hers. Janet was a little perplexed by Laura gesture, but she didn't pull away.

"I'm sure I would have loved him," Janet said, trying to sound sympathetic.

"His parents live in Montana; their names are Robert and Anne Blaine."

"I know the children told us they had grandparents in Montana. But they wouldn't tell us their names."

Laura smiled faintly and said, "That was one of the rules of the game, not to tell."

Still perplexed, Janet was relieved when Laura quickly continued.

"I just found out that my husband was adopted by Robert and Anne Blaine," said Laura. She took one of her hands away from Janet's hand and reached into her skirt pocket and pulled out the yellowed envelope. Laura looked into Janet's eyes and even before she spoke tears were forming in her eyes again.

Janet was getting more confused with the way this woman was carrying on.

"Anne sent me this letter. I know about the little boy you had to give up at birth," Laura said.

Janet was stunned and pulled back her hand from Laura's. "Who told you that?" Janet demanded.

"Mr. Chapman told me," Laura confessed.

"Why would he tell you—a complete stranger? Our own children don't even know."

"Janet, please don't be angry, he did it for a good reason."

But Janet was furious. "What good reason could that be?" she snapped.

"I know you gave up your little boy because you wanted a better life for him. That must have broken your heart."

"It did break my heart. And my heart is still breaking," said Janet. "But what does that have to do with you and why would Warren tell you my personal affairs?" Janet's heart was beating fast and anger was showing on her face.

Laura could see she was not explaining things very well so she decided she needed to come right out with it. "I think my husband, Christian Blaine, is the baby boy you gave up at birth forty-three years ago."

Janet looked at Laura as if she was delusional.

"I'm not sure but maybe this letter will give us some more information." She held the envelope out to Janet.

Janet glared at Laura. "Please look at the letter," Laura pleaded.

Janet took the envelope and saw that it was addressed to Janet Douglas, but she didn't recognize the address. "I don't understand. That's my name from my first marriage, but I never lived in Montana. So this must not be for me." She held it out for Laura to take back.

"Look at the return address and the postmark," Laura said gently.

Janet read aloud, "Sacramento Adoption Agency, Sacramento, California, 1973."

Janet's face turned from anger to bewilderment. "That's the adoption agency that handled the adoption of my baby boy. Where did you get this?" Janet asked faintly.

"Anne Blaine sent it to me. She's the woman who adopted my husband."

Janet was speechless and just listened to what Laura said next. "As far as Anne and I can figure out, this letter might have been delivered forty-three years ago. But because she didn't know a Janet Douglas at the time she sent it back. It must have been in the Post Office dead letter storage all these years. But for some reason it was redelivered to her. I called her Friday and that's when she told me Christian, my husband, was adopted. I told her about how Mr. Chapman thought maybe Christian was your baby boy. They have the same birthday and Dawn looks just like you at the age of twelve. She also has the same birthmark as you and your baby son. Anne received this letter the next day."

Janet was astonished. Warren came in and sat by his wife. "You knew all about this and didn't tell me?" she questioned.

"I didn't want to get your hopes up and then see your heart break if I wasn't right about my hunch. I think you had better open the letter," he coached.

"I don't want to tear it. Do you have your little pocketknife?" He smiled and took it from his pocket and handed to her. She gently inserted the blade at the top edge of the letter and slowly cut the top of the envelope. She pulled out the two papers and gently unfolded them. The first paper was a letter.

April 25, 1973
Sacramento Adoption Agency
Gerry Thomas,
Attorney at Law

Dear Mrs. Douglas,

I'm sending you a copy of the Adoption Release Form.

I send my condolences to you on the death of your husband, Dale Douglas.

You have made a responsible decision to release your baby for adoption. He has been placed with a loving family. I feel they will raise and support him with the necessities of life.

Sincerely,
Gerry Thomas

She handed the letter to Warren and looked at the other paper. It was an adoption release form. She saw the name Andrew Dale Douglas she had written where she crossed out "baby boy." She scanned down the paper and saw Dale Douglas as the father and she was listed as the mother. She saw her signature she had signed to give away her precious baby boy. Janet held the yellowed document close to her and wept softly. All these years she had wondered: was he happy, was he healthy, did his adoptive mother love him as much as she did? There were so many other things she longed to know about him. Warren put his arm around his wife; tears were also filling his eyes. Laura was caught up into the moment and she was crying, too.

Janet looked at Laura and said, "They only let me hold my baby boy for five minutes," she was still sobbing. "But I saw he had the same diamond purple birthmark I have."

"Dawn has the same birthmark," said Laura.

Enlightenment and thrill sprang to Janet's face. She looked at Laura again. "If your husband is my baby boy then your children really are my grandchildren!"

"Yes," said Laura, "my children are your grandchildren."

Janet gasped, "Oh my, I don't even know what to say!" as she dried her tears away with tissue, making room for a fresh flow of tears. "Warren, the children are really our own grandchildren!"

"Yes, they are," Warren smiled through his own tears.

Kimber came running into the room and saw her grandparents and mother wiping the tears away. She stopped in front of her mother. "Mommy, what's wrong? Are you okay?"

Janet looked into the little concerned face, the very face she looked into only a few weeks ago, and thought if she had a granddaughter she wanted her to be just like this little girl. "Everything is wonderful," Janet said, "Nothing could be better, Kimber. Nothing in the whole wide world."

Epilogue

By Dawn Blaine:

We never know where life is going to take us. And sometimes we have surprises we never knew awaited us, connections we never knew would change our lives forever. One decision can ultimately change everything. Some call it coincidence. Some call it fate. What would *you* call it? But for me, Dawn Elizabeth Blaine, I think my daddy had something to do with it.

Acknowledgements

One of my favorite movies has always been The Parent Trap. The idea for *Grandparent Trap* first came to me in the 1980s. When I became a grandmother I began working on the story in earnest, finally completing it after my retirement.

I want to thank Kimberly M for doing the first read and editing of the book. I will always love her for that and she will get the first book off the press.

I thank my three daughters, April, Laura and Dawn for helping with the cost of publishing of the book. I especially thank Laura who, when hearing the idea for the book, kept after me to write and finish it. Without their encouragement and financial support this book would not be.

Also to all my friends that read the book and said I should publish it, I thank you.

I want to thank Lauren and Judy Ball for their input, advice and extreme patience in making this book happen.

Lastly, thanks to all the people who bought and took the time to read my book. May God bless you all.

Carollee Young

Carollee married and raised her family in the Sacramento, California area and now lives in the foothills near Yosemite National Park. She has three daughters, one granddaughter, and one great granddaughter. Carollee is active in her church and is happiest when surrounded by family.

You can learn more about Carollee, download some of her short stories, and find out when her next books are coming out by visiting her website: **www.carolleeyoungauthor.com**

CPSIA information can be obtained
at www.ICGtesting.com
Printed in the USA
JSHW030836050420
4994JS00002BA/420

The Christmas Elves' Story

It was the middle of July, and the North Pole elves were already bustling with Christmas preparations. The workshop buzzed with activity as they joyfully crafted toys, brimming with excitement and happiness.

The elves skillfully created dolls depicting male and female superheroes, paying close attention to intricate details. These dolls were meticulously painted, adorned with flowing capes, ready for imaginary battles in the hands of children.

In another area of the workshop, elves were busy assembling game consoles. With their nimble fingers, they skillfully connected wires and chips, transforming them into enchanting devices capable of whisking children away to various realms of play.

Beside crafting game consoles, the elves were also busy making teddy bears, bikes, toy cars, and trucks. Each toy was meticulously crafted with love and care, bringing them to life with the skilled hands of the elves.

In a special section of the workshop, there was a kitchen where elves crafted various candies. The atmosphere was filled with the sweet aroma of sugar and spices as they worked on caramel and molded chocolates.

They crafted elegant shoes and cowboy boots meticulously, with each stitch and shoelace carefully done. Their remarkable focus on details guaranteed that every child would be delighted with their presents.

In a corner that echoed like a prehistoric jungle, the elves were busy painting dinosaurs of various sizes and shapes, using vibrant colors to make them come alive.

They were also putting together fishing poles, complete with small hooks and reels. These poles were created to assist children in learning how to fish and, with any luck, catch "the Big one" someday.

At the end of the day, the elves cleaned up the workshop. Their faces radiated satisfaction and excitement, envisioning the delight and happiness their creations would bring to the children.

They envisioned the laughter, excitement, and wide-eyed wonder of Christmas morning. This joy and happiness motivated their diligent work, making each stitch and brushstroke meaningful and worthwhile.

The elves understood the immense responsibility they carried. They were the bringers of joy, the weavers of dreams. Their dedication to crafting each toy was unwavering, as they poured their heart and soul into their work.

As they drifted off to sleep, their dreams were filled with the melody of jingle bells and children's laughter. Their hearts overflowed with contentment, realizing they had spread happiness far and wide. And the next day, they would take this joyful journey again.

Mery Christmas
to You

Made in the USA
Las Vegas, NV
24 November 2024

12537066R20017